Dear Future Historian, Summer 2020

Lotous Michalopoulou

Dear Future Historian
Summer 2020

Copyright © 2020 Lotous Michalopoulou

All rights reserved. No part of this publication may be reproduced, stored in a retrieval system, or transmitted in any form or by any means, electronic, mechanical, photocopying, recording or otherwise, without the prior written permission of the author or publisher.

Written by: Lotous Michalopoulou

Contact information:

dearfuturehistorians.blogspot.com
facebook.com/Dearfuturehistorians
lotous.michalopoulou@yahoo.com

Contents

ACKNOWLEDGMENTS 7

QUOTES FOR INTRODUCTION: 9

PERSONAL DIARY ENTRIES DEDICATED TO THE DEAR FUTURE HISTORIANS. 11

Dear Future Historian 13

My sunflower lanyard 16

'Anything Worth Doing is Worth Doing Badly' 21

Red-eyes-evil characters in cartoons 25

Trigger alert: suicide & mental health issues 27

Whatever 32

June 21st 34

Anxiety 35

Be kind to children to change the world 37

Lotus 41

Book review (Elementation) 43

'We are all stories in the end, just make it a good one' 46

Inherited guilt 50

Start over and over again... and again 53

Fighting the Dragon of Chaos 56

- Short stories 60
- I love the Moon 62
- London, Sisyphus... and my legs hurt 64
- Solipsistic pasta 70
- Ants, soda powder and Laura Clery 72
- What's wrong with me? 74
- 13th or 14th of July 2020 77
- Weeping angels' survivors 79
- My autism diagnosis is finally official! 84
- Intergalactic cable, or penguins? 87
- Post-diagnosis 92
- Existential terror crises 96
- My self-diagnosis notes 100
- Adulting (and support network) 105
- Thoughts of Immortality 108
- Tough love 113
- Interconnection, though-out history 117
- 'Every choice reveals what we think a human being should be' 121
- Some more Sartre 124
- On free will 129

Miracle engineering 134

My weirdest story 139

On dreams 147

Stay safe and take care 155

SHORT STORIES, POEMS AND A SCRIPT.. 157

Are you reading what I am writing, or am I writing what you are reading? 159

Cosmogony myth and gods' family dysfunction 163

The 'ultimate Truth' 169

Thinking-ourselves-into-existence 178

Good morning Sun 181

'Salvation' 185

Poem: If all the MEs 193

Poem: The lost girl 195

'DIY' (Do It Yourself) - short story script 199

About the author: 211

Acknowledgments

This book is dedicated

to the Dear Future Historians,

to my devoted contemporary readers, and

to you; who'd like to read

my personal stories and thoughts, and won't let

my dyslexia mistakes,

my English-is-not-my-first-language-barrier, or

my lack of editor stop you.

                                          Thank you for existing.

Quotes for Introduction:

'Any philosophy that accepts death must itself be considered dead, it's questions meaningless, it's consolations worn out'

Alan Harrington

'He who has ears, let him hear.'

Matthew 11:15

'Dear Future Historian,'

Personal diary entries dedicated to the dear future Historians.

(*This was my first 'Dear future Historian,' for a creative writing assignment at uni, and how I got the idea for my blog.)

*4/14/2020

Dear Future Historian

02/02/2020   02:02am   Canterbury   UK

Dear Future Historian:

First global palindrome day in 909 years!

Came home from work at 10:30pm and I'm sleepy since midnight, but I promised to myself I will be awake at 02:02. Not sure exactly what I had in mind; but, thanx to Netflix and wine, here I am. So… cheers, I guess.
May we watch series and drink wine in 03/03/3030.

05/02/2020   10:15pm   Canterbury   UK

Dear Future Historian:

I just love Uni! Now I have a referenceable, academic, source to explain the mess in my house.
'It seems as if being out of their own homes has made them lose all interest in any housework.' (It's from a housewife's diary, from the 2nd world war, about the 'evacuees').
Yet, my dear Diary, Freeman was again like: 'Don't talk rubbish'.
But I totally make sense. I mean… Dah! So, I was like: 'The mess, the un-decorated walls, the un-matched pillowcases, and the endless piles of dishes. Everything. I need my own house. That's it. Mine! In my name. One I can paint the walls rainbow, and put frames on the walls, and my Tardis clock… on the wall. My own 4 walls. Need a roof too. Maybe then I will hoover behind the sofa. Maybe then I'll bake you a cake from scratch. In my oven!'

08/02/2020   07:21pm   Margate   UK

Dear Future Historian:

A quiet day with the kids.
We went to Margate and saw a mesmerizing sunset. A flock of birds, colours, clouds, the sound of the waves.
I watched a video on YouTube, one of a psychology professor's lectures. He pointed out how important is to 'clean your room'. Then I remembered mum's Feng Shui books.
'Always be responsible and grateful, my dear', mum 'always' say... Right? I hate it when she says that. 'Be present in the Here and Now'. Maybe she's right!! (Never thought I'd say that).

11/02/2020   01:10pm   Canterbury   UK

Dear Future Historian:
Today, scrolling on FB, I read an article about how much social media and press influence our opinions and life views.
So... Bravo, my dear diary, well done. I hate you!
Cause I get now what mum meant when she insisted that 'keeping a diary is the only way to keep sane'.
Which also means I better go wash the dishes now.

11/02/2020   10:10pm   Canterbury   UK

I finished the dishes!!!
It took me like... forever.
I had headphones and was listening to an audiobook.

My sunflower lanyard

18/04/2020 Canterbury UK 07:38 pm

Dear Future Historian,

Every time I go to the supermarket with my sunflower lanyard it is a completely different experience than without it. I am the same. But the people's attitude towards me is suddenly altered. No more 'what's wrong with you' looks. No more 'another immigrant that can't speak English' looks. (I stutter when I have social anxiety, and when I came to the UK, I became even more self-aware of my speech, which increases my anxiety to levels that it looks like I can't even speak English). One could argue about my inadequate level of English, or about the disability aspect of my autism.

Yet my sunflower lanyard transfers me to a world that people are nice to me, without minding about my struggles. A world that I am accepted, and smiled by the cashier, and reassured that I don't need to stress if I don't have all my groceries in bags before the receipt is out. And the magical key to this Utopia? My beautiful sunflower lanyard, reminding me of my favourite painter, and my favourite Doctor Who episode. What a bliss to be able to walk about the supermarket corridors and take forever to choose which tea bags to get. Sounds perfect, right?

My dear future Historian... you already know the answer, don't you? Sitting there, with your godly omniscient. Pretending that you will never get an insight into our time. Yet, we both know that you know more than I ever will. (Except if my immortality quest is successful, in which case I am probably the brunet in your team, pretending to study Me, making sure that I monitor the interpretations of my work). You know that the Jews, before the Holocaust, were forced to wear the Star of David, long before they were put in those trains to concentration camps. (Wow, that escalated fast/quickly/unexpectedly).

Yeah, I know. It is not the same. This is not forced upon me. I asked for it. I took a deep breath, and I managed to ask for one, from customer service (I get very nervous talking to people I don't know, and I always avoid interaction with staff). So, since I got in so much trouble for it, and it makes such a difference to my shopping experience... why do I keep freaking out with the idea that people need me to get voluntarily vulnerable, in order to be nice to be? On the other hand, why do I have to announce my inefficiencies, to feel like a 'normal' human being?

Now with the lock-down, it's crazy. But not just the parts everyone talks about. The craziest part is that I was diagnosed with OCD. A disorder, right? And now the government advice is to do all this... that forced upon me yet another label. 'Wash your hands all the time, don't touch anything without fantasizing the potential hidden/microscopic enemies, clean the ice-cream box with chlorine before you put in in the freezer, freak out about hygiene in public transport. So now who is the crazy one?

Why should I be the one stepping out, for everyone to see my sunflowers (I love how the lanyard looks), and why we don't agree, as a society, for people that - won't be nice to you if you don't agree to be labelled 'disable' - for them to wear a lanyard?

They said on the radio, if you have any thoughts or feelings that make you struggle, if you are depressed or anything like that you should talk about it. People always say that, but they don't mean it. Even if they do, they don't really know how to react to people in need of comfort and reassurances. It is then that need to be educated how to listen. People in need always wants to talk. That is not the issue. The real challenge of the system is how to educate them to listen.

It is the same with 'laziness'. Family and friends judge people for not being productive. But if you accept a diagnosis, and (preferably) some kind of medication, then you get support and understanding. Teenagers are punished for their mental health issues. Autistic kids are punished for their meltdowns. Working people are excluded from the 'brake socialization'. 'But don't feel bad. All that is perfectly civilized, because they can just 'come out of the closet', for them to get all the support they need (with the appropriate monitoring that that goes with).

And again, only you, my dear future Historian could tell me, if those sunflowers will end us up in some other, metaphorical (or not!), train to isolation/extinction· or the lanyard will help in autism/mental-health/hidden-disabilities awareness.

I need to go now. Talk to you soon.

'Anything Worth Doing is Worth Doing Badly'

19/05/2020

Dear future historian,

As you might know I published my first book on Amazon. In a way it was like what Jordan Peterson say: 'Anything Worth Doing is Worth Doing Badly'. https://youtu.be/FJV7HeHT4q4

I had many layout and other issues because I didn't use a template in the beginning. Not that I didn't know I should. But... I forgot! The thing is I let these things stop me up until now. But as much as I have my differences with some of Peterson's opinions - mostly about child raising, and his refusal to see the reality of women's depression though out history- I can't but admit that his message has changed my life.

It took me two weeks to solve my layout issues, because I additionally suddenly had Office Word problems, with my laptop! I took deep breaths, I hugged trees, I meditated on the water and the Sun. All these techniques that I had already, for almost two decades, in my Elementation book, written 10 years ago and then forgotten. The fear of failure and my perfectionism had paralyzed me.

And then, in 2018, I heard Dr Jordan Peterson saying, 'Anything Worth Doing is Worth Doing Badly'. I watched his entire Biblical series. 'Maps of Meaning' (at first on YouTube and then Audible), 'Personality and its transformations'; I read '12 rules for Life' and got his 'Future Authoring Program.'

Still, I had to wait for the pandemic, that filled the social media with people hugging trees, to cope with social distancing rules.
And one morning I knew that it was time for me to publish the book; gaining my confidence from the power of this techniques, instead of my imaginary will-have-somehow-one-day perfection.

Perfection is a process. You can't start your journey if you don't even take the first step. So, when the technical issues occurred, I didn't have the illusion anymore that it could, or even should, be perfect. I surly spend days trying to fix it. I did the best I could. And I did eventually manage -with the help of my friend and editor, Jay Leonard Schwartz- to fix them. But I didn't have any more the naivety to think that I was the only one that didn't know, before actually learning.

Being autistic, for most of my life undiagnosed, I am prone to anxiety and self-blame. Each autistic person is different. But most of us face similar difficulties. The Elementation techniques has helped me to survive my undiagnosed era. After years of struggle, when I found out about my autism, I was finally able to deal with my sensory overload, since before I didn't even have the knowledge to identify it.

But it was only after Peterson shifted my mind and lifted the burden of my fear of failure, that I was able to take the first step. I registered with the Open University, in 2018. And now I am finally sharing with you my techniques, having the confidence in their power to balance your energy levels and connect you with Nature. I wish, future historian, that you could answer me back.

But this message, is more towards my contemporary citizens of the World. With the hope that we will take the first steps, that will hopefully lead to a place we'll be proud to have provided for you, my dear future historian. A World of Meaning.

And the only think I can say to everyone that bought my book, before I managed to change the layout, is… well, I hope that I will became known enough one day, to give you the opportunity to bit it on eBay, as a rare, first edition copy. Thank you all for supporting me.

Find the full biblical studies of Jordan Peterson at: https://www.youtube.com/watch?v=f-wWBGo6a2w&list=PL22J3VaeABQD_IZs7y60I3lUrrFTzkpat

Red-eyes-evil characters in cartoons

Dear future historian,

28/05/2020

Has people spotted yet in your time the fact that red-eyes-evil characters in cartoons promote skin colour racism?
I noticed that my 6-year-old is really convinced that all bad guys can be spotted by their eye colour.

I don't even know where to start with that!

That stereotype first of all tricks children into the idea that malevolence is spottable.

Which would be ideal, and quite convenient; yet as we all adults know, angel-eyes are not an indication of innocence. I don't feel our children are safe if they believe that there is an arrow pointing dangerous people.

Second, red-eye's stereotype seems like an initiation into the idea that skin -or eye- colour differences indicate intentions. I am so surprise no one talks about that.

I am also very sleepy.

So, talk latter my dear future historian.

I have to sleep so my son won't think in the morning that I am possessed by evil, because I will have red-sleepy-eyes.

I hope you live in a word that skin and neurodiversity are celebrated, and people won't 'believe', with such a reverence, in group-identity; I hope they realize that everyone is unique.

Talk soon.

Trigger alert: suicide & mental health issues

17/06/2020

Dear Future Historian,

I need to talk, even if it's been 13 years.
At the cemetery. Everyone is dead here. Everyone but me. A cat suddenly appears from behind a grave. I keep walking. At some point, I reach John's grave.
'Hi mate, I told you I'd come'.
I take off my shoes. Graves are holy ground. I place the sleeping bag on and sit down. Next, I take the bottle of wine that I had brought and open it.
'Cheers John'. I drink a bit, then I get up, lift the sleeping bag, and pour some wine on his grave.

'Cheers'.
I was about to drink some more wine, but then I thought that I would need a wee soon. I have a long night ahead of me. The cold is getting stronger. I lay in my cocoon, on the grave, when I thought I heard footsteps. I jump up. Well if it was a ghost then John could also become a ghost and he'd protect me. Maybe.
'Will you ever forgive me mate for... for letting this happen?'
I only knew him for three months. And at first, he was more into my sister anyway. But I was recovering from a break-up. And we had the best 3 months ever. Or it would have been if I wasn't still in love with my ex.
Then Autumn came, along with my ex. He wanted me back, I wanted him back.
I hated him.

'Why now? Now that I have to break someone's heart to be with him. Maybe I have to stay with John now; maybe we will outlive John and get back together in the far future, after he is… not-here-any-more.'
That was of course never the plan. That was just a thought. A fast disposable thought. But, not fast enough for me not to remember that it did indeed cross my mind just three days before John jumped out of a mental hospital window!
I was grumpy that weekend. My ex met me to ask me for a goodbye-coffee before he went backpacking in Italy. John realized my mind was elsewhere and started acting weird. I said I needed some time to process all that, how I felt and what I wanted. I wanted to go backpacking too.

John mentioned death wishes. He was saying stuff about the devil, and magic ceremonies he had participated in as a teenager. He thought that his soul was doomed and that he brought misfortune to his family. I wasn't in the mood for helping anyone. I needed help myself. I wanted everyone to leave me alone.

'What the heck mate? I've told you my ex was about to kill himself some months ago. And that I only recently recovered from my religious upbringing. And now you tell me about suicide and the devil?'

I didn't say all of that of, course. I just said something like:

'Jesus can save you, even though I don't believe in any of that anymore. But if the devil exists, then so does Jesus, I guess. I know people that can help you. Let's talk about it on Monday.'

And then I left him. I just like that opened the door and left, telling myself that I can't save everyone.

'I'm just a bisexual, weird girl, with dyslexia, depression and anxiety. Why do I have to save the world?'

That was the last time I saw him. He went to a church that night. It was locked. He freaked out and some neighbors called the police. They took him to a mental hospital. He managed to break some bars and jump out of the window.

There, laying upon John's grave, I promise that I will never underestimate the power of my help and my energy again. I could have helped him, or at least I could have tried. I did know people that could actually help him. But I thought it wasn't my job to save him. I thought that I could demand from the universe a weekend off, to think through my own problems.
I'm cold and I need a wee even more now. The shadows are spooky and no sign of the cat. I sit up again and as I turn to take the wine bottle, I see her, the Moon. She's always there for me, always keeping me company.

I am suddenly aware that I am at a cemetery for real. I get in my sleeping bag again and I close my eyes.
I start the mantra that my Google search guaranteed would give me access to the 5th dimension, the place of dreams and the dead. I add a little bit of Carlos Castaneda and the books, the movies and the Greek myths that I know, about contacting the dead.

That's what I came to do tonight. Try to contact John for the last time. Tell him I'm sorry that I didn't even try to save him. And promise him that I will never shut my door to my friends again. He was my friend.
Mumbling the mantra, and despite the fact that I want to wee, I'm cold, and in a cemetery, I fall asleep imagining my funeral. I want to be re-born. Not in the Christian way. In my way. I want to be the one that will try to save the world. I want to always have my door open to my friends and I want my books to affect people, to help them choose life. Back to the mantra.

At 5 am I wake up. I need to go before people start coming. I pack up. I don't remember my dream. Maybe John heard my apology even if I didn't hear him. Maybe I wasn't worthy to go to the 5th dimension in full awareness.

Maybe I'm just getting on the same catastrophic track as he did. Feeling that I am not good for the people I care for. Feeling guilty led him to the grave.

Maybe It will help if I write about it.

Maybe... I don't know.

PS. The cover of this book is photo* of a wall-collage I made when John died, to keep me sane. You can find more photos of this project @
https://dearfuturehistorians.blogspot.com/2020/04/collage-attempts-2002-2012.html

*by Christina Christidou.

Whatever

18/06/2020

Dear future historian,

I wrote that many hours ago... but I wasn't sure if I should share it.
At the end I thought that... what's the point of writing if I am not honest with who I am?
So... here it is:

I am so so upset!

On autistic pride day... the 1st year that I ever can say that I know and am proud of being autistic, I had an old classmate telling me that: it is sad that they -who are they?- convinced me that I have autism -I don't have it, it's not a chickenpox, I AM autistic- and it is also a disease that I am bisexual!' He even offered to 'help' me overcome these twisted identities... with proper diet!
Wow
I mean... whatever.
One of the reasons I am happy I don't live any more in Greece and I don't raise my kids there.
I could never be myself there. It's so sad.
Thank you for welcoming us here UK. Thank you for helping me find myself.
Happy autistic pride day 2020.
Happy pride month.

June 21ˢᵗ

Dear future historian,

Today was the longest day of the year.
I went out and hugged a beautiful tree, Tree-meditated; and I stayed out till the sunset to Sun-meditate.
'Beauty Will Save the World', said Dostoevsky.
I understand the importance of this more and more every year.
May beauty save the World, so you will live in a world that we can be proud to have given you.
Good night my dear future historian.
Stay safe and take care.

Anxiety

Image made by Christina Christidou

22/06/2020

Dear future historian,

Have I told you how I panic over everything?
My day starts with a list, unrealistically long, and it ends with frustration at the un-checked tasks.
Why don't I readjust the length of the list? I thought you'd ask me that. My dear dear, naive, future historian.
I don't know if you live with AI house-robots, or in a post-apocalyptic scenario of the future, but a to-do list of people in 2020 is crazy.
Add uni and 2 kids and the expectations are beyond the 24 hours of the day.
Now... add autism, OCD, ADHD and dyspraxia symptoms, and BAMM! You got yourself a recipe for anxiety.

I do try. And I do get better at my planning skills.
I could get into more detail about how I lack the skill to adjust quickly in transition between tasks, or my lack of consecration when I get interrupted; but then I should also elaborate on my superpowers of super-consecration, or my attention to detail and other abilities that accompany the struggles of neurodiversity. But there is already plenty of bibliography for these matters.
So, the main purpose of me telling you all that today is to let you know that the days when I don't write to you much, or even at all, please forgive me, my dear future historian. And know that am always thinking about you and my contemporary readers.
Stay safe and take care.

Be kind to children to change the world

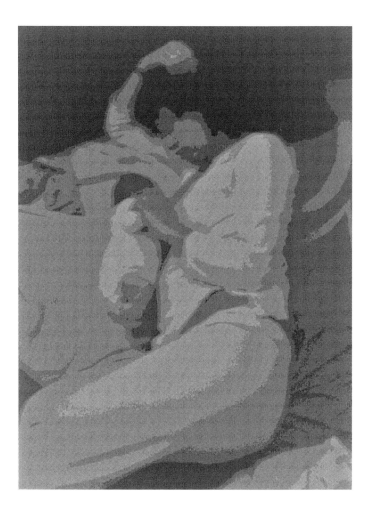

23/06/2020

Dear future historian,

Let's see... where to start here? I read, some days ago, a book 'The explosive child' (by Ross W Greene PhD) ... and I feel so ready to explode (a 'must read' book.) It's unbelievable how in the West we pathologies our most brilliant minds, medicating them to 'normalize' them. We then fill them with unrealistic expectations and on top we blame them for not fulfilling these expectations. And we never listen to their objections, we only name their reactions with offensive words, like meltdowns or disorders.

Suppressed anger leads to aggregation. Anger is a valid feeling. But anger is, for some reason, considered uncivilized. Yet censorship in anger is what brings most meltdowns. People think meltdowns are random. They are totally not. Yes... sensory issues management can help and feeling overwhelmed, tired and hungry can actually trigger meltdowns.

But usually before a meltdown there is an attempt to express the angry feelings, or an existential terror. On the other hand, an attempt to suppress and restrict, either actively or by just dismissing them, these attempts are what's causing the exposition usually.

And then Sam Harris https://samharris.org/
describes a guru in the East, that had an existential crisis at 16, laying on the floor, unresponsive for hours. But he wasn't medicated or taken to a mental institution, he was in a society that honors the ones that 'see' something that most don't, and that troubled boy became a guru.

So... what's wrong with us?

The explosive child had to dedicate a whole part on explaining to the parents that it's normal for their child to feel some foods are disgusting! And how dismissing their needs and feelings leads to unmanageable behavior. People need to actually have someone tell them this thinks!

Dayna Martin, a children's advocate
https://daynamartin.com/
https://www.amazon.co.uk/dp/0648430324/ref=cm_sw_r_cp_apa_i_P4L8Eb3TEX4WZ,
came in my life exactly when I needed her. Like she was a manifestation of a need's fulfilment, more than a real person. What was important for me was to read my thoughts written on paper, or spoken in a video, from a person in the other side of the world. She helped me having trust to my inner voice mother instincts, in a society that thinks attachment parenting is spoiling your kids. But her book was proved to be insufficient evidence for the ones that think 'kids do well if they want.' I had to find someone with Ph.D. and decades of experience in 'respectable' institutions, to be listened finally.

Why? Why people need someone with a Ph.D. to tell them they should be nice to their children?
My dear future historian, please tell me that at least in your time people get it. I know the environmental disaster, and racism, and wars, is how people measure our negative progress. But I do see people being at least nicer to their kids as parents in the 80s where, or at least try to be, or at least watch shows that expect them to be. I see a progress that gives me some kind of optimism.

And then I read books like that, and have that bittersweet feelings of, it is nice that someone with 'authority' finally talks about these things... and at the same time, why these thinks even need to be debated? Why the need for logical arguments on 'you have to treat your children with kindness and trust that they are doing their best?'

https://www.livesinthebalance.org/step-one-first-video

My dear future historian... just please, if we don't make it, I leave it in your hands, to make sure that people will finally learn to be kind, the way the Capaldi Doctor would say.

'Hate is always foolish, and love is always wise. Always try to be nice, but never fail to be kind.'

https://youtu.be/yJqsPBWbtjk

Lotus

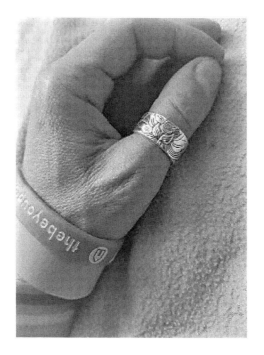

25/06/2020

Hello dear future historian,

Just a quick thought today, to show you my new ring. You know... my childhood self-hated my Lotus name. I would get so upset if I knew that I would proudly wear that ring!

In Greece people can't even pronounce it (which makes even more ironic the fact that now people can't pronounce my last name, here in the UK. :-p And why did they write it with 'ou' on my Greek passport anyway? What does 'Lotous' suppose to mean?)

Long story short, going to a public school with that name, was like having a tattoo on my forehead, saying: 'bully me.'

But... as we all know... Lotus (and maybe even Lotous) might grow in the mud... but that doesn't stop a Lotus to get its full glory.

So... here I am... a proud Lotus... with a ring.

Sorry my dear childhood me

At least I wrote a book, as I promised you. And I am writing another one. ;-)

Take care and stay safe my dear future historian.

Always remember the child you were. (Sorry if you are a clone and that is offensive.)

Book review (Elementation)

26/062020

Dear future historian,

Wow. Today I got the best review that I could possibly hope for my book!
And you know from whom?

Remember Dayna Martin? The unschooler writer, children's advocate, etc, that I follow for more than a decade (that I mentioned on the 23rd of June?) A real role model for me, for years now.
Yes! Actually, really, unbelievably... from her! Definitely a big even to write about in my diary.
May all the big events for me, you, and my contemporary readers be as positive as this one, my dear future historian.

(The review:)

'Really inspiring book!

I like to consider myself a seasoned new-age seeker, and I thought that this book would be sort of a review of what I already knew. Boy... was I wrong! I learned so much from this book that inspired me the moment after I finished it! I went outside to find a tree to introduce myself to, connect with, and touch. I also began looking for rocks on the ground to pick up and hold to connect with their energy.

I could tell that the author put a great deal of research into what she was writing about, and her passion for "Elementation" (new word for me) was so inspiring!

During these uncertain times having another tool to help you cope with stress and fear is always welcome! This book encourages you to look at what's all around you and tap into the healing energy just waiting to help you with anxiety, depression, and stress.

I'm so grateful for what I've learned in this book and I hope others get just as much out of it as I did!

We need to collectively heal to help shift the world towards more peace, love, and compassion.
This book shows you how.'

https://www.amazon.com/gp/aw/d/B087SHC1MM/ref=tmm_pap_title_0?ie=UTF8&qid=&sr=

PS. I am making a new cover for the book, and also the audiobook is done, my narrator finished recording and now we are waiting for it to be released by Audible.

'We are all stories in the end, just make it a good one'

28/06/2020

Dear future historian,

Today feels weird. Not sure why.
A mix of too much and nothingness, boredom and stress, overload and not enough stimulation.

It took me like forever to make an add on Facebook for my book. Then I spend some time contemplating on how unrelated you are, my dear future historian, with my book, and how confusing it might be for my Facebook page visitors to see my letters to you, when my 'buy now' button is a mindfulness book. And after that most of my 'free-time' was spend on 'kitchen trips' in search for snacks -that I ending up not eating, because I get anorexic when I'm stressed- and some ADHDing (as I use to call that, like going up and down for no specific reason.) In general, a lot of disappointment on myself and a lot of doubt on my life's and marketing's skills.

Well, that was till I saw my sister's documentary, again, about the villages the Nazi's burned in Greece during the second world war! (https://youtu.be/-8czrIriWJQ and http://lightthickens.eu/) With people that where there and are still alive, talking about their memories. Real people.
I mean, I usually think of the second world war like in a history book; not unlike the first world war, or the Middle Ages, or the Parthenon, for that matter. We are supposed to not really make the distinction between real people, real stories and the mytho-poetic realm (I love it when Jason Silva talks about the myhto-poetic https://www.facebook.com/jasonlsilva/?epa=SEARCH_BOX.) And that is an evolutionary tool, that we humans have, in one hand. It helps us see the meta-stories (as Peterson points out

https://www.youtube.com/watch?v=RudKmwzDpNY) and gain 'experience' and coping mechanism strategies, that our lifetime duration is not enough to have developed by ourselves. That power of stories brings me always in a state of Awe.

Yet, on the other hand, yesterday I realized that even me -that I have such a passion for narratives- do have a kind of distinction in my head between what we call 'reality' and the realms of mythical heroes. Not only that, but in these 'alternative universes' is where I store information about historical, far away in time, events. And even if my brain fails, as they say, to realize the difference between real danger and a horror movie, I spotted yesterday -in my surprise that some word war two survivors are still alive- a whispering that tells me that the heroes of the mytho-poetic are no comparison with real people.

As if a catastrophe might be a good opportunity for a mythical hero to become a legend, but... 'let's not fool ourselves, that is not the case with real people; real people get PTSD, and possibly die out of too much stress hormones or something.' Otherwise why was I so surprised to see survivors of the second world war, being still alive to see the internet and smart watches? It all comes to the 'story we tell ourselves, about ourselves,' about our lives. 'We are all stories in the end, just make it a good one' as the Doctor (Doctor Who) said
(https://www.youtube.com/watch?v=gdXLCDdn48s&t=79s.)

We can be victims of... whatever. Or we can call ourselves 'survivors.' We can be the 'heroes' that you, my friend dear future Historian, will have to try to comprehend how 'real' we are, and at the same time how much like mytho-poetic heroes, in order for you to allow yourself to not be a victim of 'whateverness,' but a survivor of anything that you might worry it will undermine your life expectancy.

May my writings help you, and me, realize the heroic potential in all of us. Stay safe and take care.

Inherited guilt

30/06/2020

Dear future historian,

Sorry. I had two days of going out for post office, grocery shopping and stuff... and I just didn't find any time to write to you. This lockdown made me realize how much energy I loose when I go out with a 'to do list' and how happy I am at home. (At least I hugged a Tree.)
I... how can I tell you that?

Well, just some days before the pandemic was known and the lockdown was a thing, I wished to stay home for 6 months. I just felt exhausted, and I could tell that I needed a break.

The only thing at the moment that 'reassures' me that my wish was not the cause of the coronavirus is the fact that it started some months before we found out about it, before my wish.

But then the Doctor starts his time-y wimey https://youtu.be/q2nNzNo_Xps so then its again hard to eliminate completely the possibility of my responsibility for the pandemic.

It's also Jordan Peterson's https://www.youtube.com/playlist?list=PL22J3VaeABQD_IZs7y60I3lUrrFTzkpat lectures about responsibility, the biblical notion of catastrophes being linked to it and how this idea led to the 'cause and effect' mindset that helped the West reach the Enlightenment.

So... maybe it is my fault somehow. Or maybe the Christian idea of inherited guilt is so deep in me that I still can't get rid of.

Either way maybe I should just enjoy my calmness while I still have the chance to stay inside.

But you know by now, my dear future historian (even if my contemporaries don't know yet, that I will write one day a book called 'How to overthink properly') my love for 'proper overthinking.'

Whether I do it continuously or not it will happen anyway. Better not without me.

Better if I try to give it a push so it won't be in circles, but it will start unravelling all the unjustified guilt that my upbringing has left me.

I need a coffee.
I'll go read something religious to stay in climate. :-p
Talk later
Stay safe and take care.

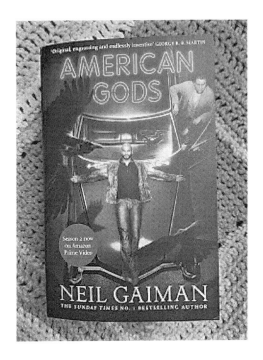

Start over and over again... and again

Photo by me. Thessaloniki, Navarinou square

01/07/2020

Dear future historian,

Some days I feel empty, like all my energy has been used. Like fatigue is stronger than me. These days I've learned to start over, to begin again.

About 10 years ago, I was living in Thessaloniki, Greece, up on hill, about 30 minutes walking distance from the center. I frequently took long walks, with my baby girl in a slink. One day I met my mum, went out for a walk in the center, then went to a play area for quite some time, then started walking up the hill, home. On the way I suddenly realized that it has been more than 6 hours since the last time I ate anything, and the baby hasn't stopped breastfeeding, and I feel like passing out. Halfway home I felt like I couldn't make another step. That was as far as my limits can take me.

I started dragging myself, and with each step I was telling to myself the story of how many hours I am walking, and then in the next step, I was adding that distance again in my head, by retelling that story. And all these steps piled up an imaginary, subconscious fake distance, that drained my energy in a logarithmic increasing way. Another advance of 'proper overthinking' is that it helps with spotting this kind of subconscious mind games.

I stopped. Took a few deep breaths. Then I decided to forget the past steps. Focus on the moment. Have a 'tourist gaze' and begin again, start over and over, on each step. As if it is the first one. The moments that my mind begged for some counting, I let it count how many steps to home, not how many we've done so far. And my energy returned. And was renewed every time I was starting over. And I got home. And my life was never the same again.

From that day I knew how to 'keep going.' And it works every time. Of course, some days I just refuse to stop telling myself the list of my reasons to assume that my energy is gone. 'It must be' my mind insists.
But it's not to trick me. Nor to harm me in any way. It's just that my mind is trained in that linear time mind-set. Where an endless source of energy is unthinkable. How can I demand my mind to think of something unthinkable?
Not to mention the inherent guilt that I mentioned yesterday. That hides behind most self-sabotage behaviors.
Sam Harris reminded me of that day.
https://api-v2.wakingup.com/player/66315d

It is times like that, my dear future historian, that I like to reassure my mind, by writing about all that. Because sometimes, it is our time to be the one telling our story, to our minds. Sometimes our minds need that. And you'll be surprised by a minds willingness to listen to a good story.

PS. Remember to tell a good inspirational story to yourself when your energy is gone, or whenever you need to.

Stay safe and take care.

Fighting the Dragon of Chaos

04/07/2020

Dear future historian,

I still haven't managed consistency with your letters... but believe me, I'm trying. I have a test next week and I'm studying. I'll tell you all about it next week. For now, I want to focus on anxiety again.

I was watching Jordan Peterson's family update video, that he did some days ago with his daughter, and part of it was his description of severe anxiety attacks and akathisia...
https://youtu.be/qQyhn9DPE00

Dear future historian, day 2.

It's actually been 3 days that am trying to write to you. The first day I didn't find any time. (Note to self: what if the goal of everyday entries is too much for me at the moment?)
Day 2, yesterday I fell asleep -3 hours before my bedtime- typing on my phone to you. And don't assume for a second that I'm bored of my 'letters' to you. But I just was so tired. I'm a bit nervous lately, and I've been going up and down a lot, so end up being very tired all the time. (Note to self: maybe write in the morning, before I get so tired...
- ...
- I know I'm not a morning type but you can't 'not be a morning person' and the fall asleep at 8:30pm...)
So... let's start over... again and again. Where were we?

Oo yeah, in Peterson fight with the Dragon of Chaos. Well. I mostly mentioned that because I was pacing a lot lately. Struggling to sit down to read and write. Even watching videos seam too static some days.
So, when Peterson and every Peterson has opinions and suggestions about why people can get out of a bad loop, or whatever... I mean, I was just wondering if in his new book -after his latest 'adventure'- he'll give more consideration into mental health issues, and how much they can affect someone's ability to fight Dragons. And people around usually make things worse, at least Peterson recognizes that.
Ok not that he hasn't talked about people's struggles.

But when he speaks about personal responsibility, sometimes, he sounded judgmental. Or maybe it's just me. Either way, these thoughts, after his new video, was a reminder of my interpretation of Jesus' Ethics. A mindset that I never found, in any Church, in my 20 years of being in many of them. Except my mum. She is the one how helped me see it.

So... words like Peterson's, about the personal responsibility for our condition, are only useful when they are used for personal encouragement.

The minute they become, or are interpreted as, a judgment -whether that is from other people or by ourselves/about ourselves- that minute they become petrifying, its then what Jesus mean by the parable of the prodigal son, or when he says: Matthew 7:4. How can you say to your brother, 'Let me take the speck out of your eye,' while there is still a beam in your own eye?'

Long story short, if I let my self-judgment perfidy me, I'll never write another word.

But on the other hand, if I don't motivate myself with the knowledge that I can indeed fight Dragons... then I won't write another word.

It's a matter of balance I suppose.

But it is not easy.

It's not easy my dear future historian to find that balance.

Many times, it's just that BoJack feeling left...

https://youtu.be/qQyhn9DPE00

I mean sometimes, the people around us... fail to - absorbed by, or in an attempt to get away of, their own problems- help us find the best in us. In days like this I find that stories help the most... to restore faith in humanity and myself.

And... well... then I begin again... hug a Tree and start over. Fighting the Dragons.

P.S. I. The new cover of my book just arrived.
It looks amazing. It is totally elevating looking through these trees. I love it.
https://www.amazon.co.uk/dp/B087SHC1MM/ref=cm_sw_r_cp_apa_i_W0jaFbJQ2KCDT

P.S. II. I need to finally make a realistic plan for you, my dear future historian, so I can be consistent. But please give me a couple of weeks before I work on that.

P.S III. I'll try to elaborate on all that at some point, because I am not sure I make much sense atm (= 'at the moment')

Stay safe and take care.

Short stories

05/07/2020

Dear future historian,

I didn't always appreciate short stories. They left me an uncomfortable feeling, like hearing a song for the first time. I thought that they don't give me enough time to connect with the characters, emotionally, or feel that I have enough evidence to make a certain moral judgment about them.
It was only last year that I realized the ability that short stories have to teach us how to zoom and focus in the moment, in the 'Here and Now.'
Plus, I feel lately that I just can't make a long-term commitment to a story atm. You see, I always spend a lot of time thinking of the characters and the plot of any novel I read. But now I have to focus on other things, quite a lot of things.

So... I got myself a short stories book, from one of my uni-mates. She just finished the creative writing module that I will start in the new academic year. Her book is a real inspiration. Totally recommend it.
https://www.amazon.co.uk/dp/B089M2H3QS/ref=cm_sw_r_cp_apa_i_NgoaFbFEV3MFT
So... yeah. Mostly my point today is that I denied myself for many years the joy of completing a story, by having this 'short-stories-are-not-for-me mentality, to write one. Like if my novel will get offended if I write anything else b4 (= before) I finish it.
And I was missing out on the 'Here and Now' lessons of short stories.

Here is where you come, my dear future historian. My 'letters' to you have being so therapeutic for me. Giving me, almost every day, the sense of completing and sharing something (my Here-and-Now,) to you and my contemporaries.

Thank you so much for give me a motivation to write again... even if I am not ready to complete my novel yet. Even if I'm not ready to commit to a schedule with you yet. Stay safe and take care

P.S If you enjoy poems, I recommend my other unimate's poem collection. As I said in my review:
Easy read poems dealing with deep subjects
I read these lovely poems in one go.
They made me think and weep and laugh.
https://www.amazon.co.uk/dp/B08BWFVY6L/ref=cm_sw_r_cp_apa_i_DzzaFbJ2QG0CK

I love the Moon

The Moon last night

07/072020

Dear future historian,

I have to travel to London in 2 days. During a pandemic!
Like, what if the Doctor was coming with the Tardis, and she landed in London during the Black death, or something.
It's like...

Dear future historian,

I have to travel to London tomorrow! During the pandemic. And I haven't seen the Tardis yet.

Yesterday I was interrupted, and I didn't find any time later to write to you. Even now I have to leave you. I will try to take a lot of photos and show you tomorrow, or the day after...

Lots of things to talk about, but as I read on Facebook, its mostly the things that keep me from writing, the ones I want to write about.

Talk to you soon. Stay safe and take care.

P.S. 'Over the course of one year, the 13 times that it has a full moon that is, few are the times we have the honor of seeing her. Clouds, apartment buildings, rooftops and other things usually block our beautiful round friend. Therefore, on the rare times we do meet her, it is good to stop and to pay attention to her and to give her the honor she deserves... I greet her every time I see her, whatever the stage of her cycle.'

Elementation. Hug a tree.

London, Sisyphus... and my legs hurt

09/07/2020

Dear future historian,

My legs ache so bad...

I walked so much yesterday. And I totally forgot that I haven't walked much after the lock-down. I just assumed my walking skills were waiting for me (and the World) to be ready. So, it was kind of a surprise when I woke up today and every step hurts even more than the last one.

'The rent of existence,' like to be alive you can't just 'buy your stats' and then just put them on the side, expecting them to wait for you, whenever you feel like it (feel like running, waking for miles in a day... living again among people, etc.)
It's like you need to keep paying rent, or a tax or something, constantly, or the 'stats' are reduced, maybe even taken away.

It's like Sisyphus. Walking up the mountain, carrying his rock, everyday... You know, I guess you do, you are a historian after all, that for centuries that myth was interpreted so so blindly; focusing on the punishment, on the power of the gods to put such a horrific sentence to anyone who'd even try to gain immortality.
For real, I think, it took humanity centuries, and Albert Camus' mind, to realize that Sisyphus punishment represents human condition. A seemingly pointless, endless struggle... to achieve nothing at the end. and then the next day... you have to repeat everything, all over again and again. Life is a process of carrying a huge rock up the mountain, all day, only to have to do it all over again tomorrow.

But Albert Camus realized that Sisyphus can be happy, in his daily task (not even 'despite' it.) And mostly, nobody had realized that Sisyphus indeed did gain his immortality!
He was destined to live forever, carrying his rock up the mountain -yes... only to carry it again tomorrow, but still- everyday, forever. Not in Hades, but on Earth, having a panoramic view sunset... everyday. Sounds quite immortal to me.

If I do need to carry my rock (or my cross, as Jesus suggested,) up the mountain, everyday; if I have to keep getting up every morning, brushing my teeth, doing my personal care routine... fighting the Dragons of Chaos and stuff, and somehow gain immortality in all that... then I accept (especially if my descendants may inherit immortality too (with health and youthfulness.)
I mean, you know... most people, whenever I start a conversation about the possibility of immortality, they get really uncomfortable. Years now, I do this little 'experiment.' And most people are terrified by such a thought; insisting that life is so hard, that they prefer to know it's going to end at some point.

And yet what really is hard in life is getting sick and die, you or people around you. Like, what do they mean? Like there is no chance, if one of us makes it, still no chance to spread immortality to your loved ones. Or like if the only thing that helps them get up in the morning is that at some point all this is going to end. I don't know. I don't get it. If life is hard because people get sick and die, wouldn't immortality solve the problem? So, I guess that's not really their problem. It's life itself they despite. It's that very fact of getting up in the morning and roll the rock up the hill... that is what people are most scared of. Not what might happen to them, but what is actually happening; like if what people hate is gravity itself.

Well... I love my gravity; I love my Earth. I am willing to roll the rock up the mountain... for the millennia to come.

Maybe Sisyphus found a way, after all these centuries, to build some kind of mechanism to help him release some of his heavy burden. And maybe he has a phone, or something, with broadband... and he connects to the World on his way back to the foot of the mountain, after his sunset meditation at the top... Maybe he Googles stuff, to see what the new generations write about him.

Maybe I'll find immortality, and I'll Google to see what you have to say about me, my dear future historian.

So, anyway, yesterday I went to London for my 'life in the UK test' (citizenship test), and I passed! Last weeks I was studying for it, and it was so hard for me to remember names and dates. I guess because of my dyslexia. I didn't even wanna talk about it, that's why I didn't tell you anything. I was freaking out I might panic so much at the test, and that I won't make it.

I was shaking at some point there. Like totally shivering. Like I always get when I write a test, or I'm expected to communicate something that my failure to do so, would mean something... sorry I need to go again, food is ready. Be back later.

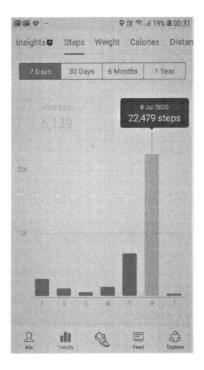

Where was I? Oh yes. I passed the test. I was freaking out before. I forget names and days. I didn't wanna talk about it. Now I'm cool... Let's change the subject. (Who said I'm still panicking for the uni test next year? Never believe these people!) And I need to stop saying 'like' so much.

P.S.1 I love London.

Note to self: I need to write about my British citizenship, Diogenes, and stuff...

Solipsistic pasta

10/07/2020

Dear future historian,

Not much today. Family time. Listening to podcasts while washing dishes and doing the laundry.

Oh, I also spent some time in my uni's philosophy forum. And... they had a topic about immortality! (I love uni.) Exploring the possibility of getting bored at some point, if you don't die! And only yesterday I was writing to you about Sisyphus. 'Is it getting Solipsistic or is it just me!' I was also thinking the other day of a kind of pasta that I liked in Greece and that I haven't found it here... next supermarket visit... I found them!

I was taught to interpret these... synchronicity events as signs that I am in some kind of 'correct path/flow,' or something like that. I don't know. I definitely hope so though. It's an extra very good time in history to be in the correct place at the correct time. Always in times of crisis this gets more vital.

Well... I'm not really in a mood to say much today.

I'm just going to leave it there.

So, stay safe and take care.

May you, and everyone who reads this, be always in the 'right place, at the right time,' whatever that means.

Ants, soda powder and Laura Clery

11/07/2020

Dear future historian,

We occupied ourselves with ants in the yard today, I made a line of bicarbonate of soda outside the door. My sister said that works for ants. It kind of did actually. It was impressive. In the beginning they seemed to be even more of them than before and there were even some with wings. But in about an hour only very few were left. So, we'll see how this goes.
Also, I got the audible of Idiot: Life Stories from the Creator of Help Helen Smash
Book by Laura Clery.

I admit washing the dished today was a pleasure listening to her (she is the narrator!) I just started it today and I already heard half of it. I just couldn't stop it.

My audible will be out soon. I didn't do the narration. First, I'm too shy at the moment for that; but even if I decided to overcome my fear, I don't have the equipment or the quite conditions to record.

It's amazing how honest Laura Clary's book is. I imagine it must have upsetted many people that are in it!

Anyway, that's it for today again.

Stay safe and take care.

Laura Clery's book:
https://www.amazon.co.uk/dp/1982101954/ref=cm_sw_r_cp_apa_i_ySHcFbDWAAZYE

What's wrong with me?

12.07/2020

Dear future historian,

There is something very weird going on with me. I don't know if it's my neurodiversity or whatever... but I noticed it yesterday.

So, I was reading a small thought experiment, not designed to make you decide or question something, just asks you to focus on you bodily sensations, as you hear a story you are supposed to star in.

It's your birthday, and the whole day is a disaster, from one unpleasant surprise to the next, but at the end your friends through you a surprise party. And... how did each incident made us feel, in our body... specifically. The practice required very detailed attention on sensations.

And then I suddenly realized... the pleasant surprise at the end... felt worse!! Like, it felt like a slap, more than when I was asked to imagine that my wallet was missing. Like if, with every obstacle in the visualization, I felt that I can still make it, I can fix it, I can work on it. But the happy surprise... that made me freeze and I had no idea how to react to such a feeling.

Not long after, mum came in the living room, and hugged me telling me -randomly- how proud she is for my book. My first thought was 'what? It's been since about May mum, you read it like... 3 times already, and you've hugged me about it like... 10 times by now.' I smiled awkwardly. Only from my kids I seem to take kind words seriously.

Anyway... I need to go. And find a way to stop sabotaging receiving love. And hug a tree.

P.S.1 Most ants are gone. I also dropped some soda powder in the middle. I am so clumsy that one third of my time in the kitchen is fixing some kind of mess I did by dropping something for example. Also, I love my new coffee-thermos-Tardis-blue thing.

P.S.2 Did you check my book yet? Did you leave a review? Did you talk with anyone about it?

https://www.amazon.co.uk/gp/product/B087SHC1MM/ref=ppx_yo_dt_b_asin_title_o00_s00?ie=UTF8&psc=1

Stay safe and take care.

13th or 14th of July 2020

Dear future historian,

Is it 13th if you haven't sleep yet, or 14th after 12am?
Not really in the mood for much today. I get that kind of blue, every time, some days after a trip. Also, a million people haven't bought my book yet, and our tickets for visiting Greece were canceled because of the pandemic.
I was listening to Steven Fry's Victorian secrets audible today... how lies in the family were a duty, rather than something negative.
How I saw it, people's mental health was unimportant, compared to social profiles.
I should write something about the Victorians at some point, combining Fry's audibles, what we did at uni, Charles Dickens, and Pirsig's: Lila...
Fry also said that it was very easy to lock someone in a mental hospital! You just had to be a family member, and not like them...
It sounds like a very hard time for neurodivers people.
Anyway... that all you'll get from me today, I guess.
That, and a random photo of my bracelets.
Stay safe and take care.

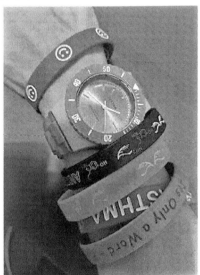

Weeping angels' survivors

15/07/2020

Dear future historian,

Remember when I went to India in 2001 (five and a half months in a biblical school?) What happened to those journals? I think there left in Greece, in my sister's shed or something. I hope you find them. So, I was remembering India today. And that woman again that I saw two men 'casting demons' out of her, by shaking her head, violently, and blaming her screams to the demons, not their harassment. That was the moment of...

Ok... so yesterday I was interrupted again and then I fell asleep early, so I didn't make my daily - unspoken- promise for 'a-post-a-day.' Well, I suppose it was a smart move to not actually say out loud that promise. There is something in failing promises that damages people's souls, in way. It makes us not trust our own self. A terrible outcome, if you consider that we are the writers of our own life.

I know many people, Sam Harris (whom I really respect) is one of them, don't believe in this kind of hocus pocus ideas...

But if we give any kind of trust in statistics... we should pay attention to all other inexplicable things too.

To me it's so obvious that our thoughts effect our reality and that we do have free will. And that all that are actually only potentials... and we have to be present and focused to actually see the results and ever to just really be.

We stay in the potentially face, not even existing for real... and then we wonder why videos are so random on YouTube, when we can just type the video we like. A life full of random playlists is not a proof that the search bar is not there.

Anyway... back to my yesterday's unfinished pattern of thought.

What strikes me always with history, the parts that are so obvious absurd for us today, life slavery and women's place, hygiene and stuff like that...

I was always wondering how difficult it must have been for the few people, ahead of their time, that could so clearly see these events how we see them. But they had to live in that timeline. Like if a weeping angel left them there (Doctor who reference.)

Maybe because I could see in the 80's how crazy those eyebrows were, or maybe it was the decorations of the degenerated stores fighting their survival from the first big supermarkets, or something like that.

I remember walking about the city center and wandering why everything was so

Ok... 2nd interruption. Where were we? You see, this is why you are my only solution atm (at the moment) my dear future historian. It's hard for me to write something more coherent that a diary, when I still don't have my own room to work. Anyway. I guess I have to manifest a room... Let's see.

I was talking about the 80's and India, right?

Basically, my point was a memorial... to all the unknown people through history, that were ahead of their time, and could clearly 'see' the absurdity of their contemporaries.

That 'exorcism' was so clearly artificial, so undoubtedly an abuse... yet it took me two more years to leave church.

It's so hard to balance the voices of peer pressure... most by dead people... with the voice of our own interpretations of the World.

When we are (so obviously for us) been treated unfairly, or we witness someone else being harassed... what could I, a 19-year-old foreigner girl do to 'save' that woman that even herself seemed to believe that he resistance was demonic?

As for me? My entire World, my whole cosmo-theory was collapsed with the earthquake that the shaking of that woman's head... manifested in mine.

How could I help her, when I needed first aids myself?

For years I was carrying the burden for not stepping up that day.

I spend 2 years in therapy after India. I had to rebuild not just my life but also my Universe, my view of the World.

Today I believe that I couldn't really do anything that day. And I should have never blamed myself for centuries of women oppression and religious superstition. That's a burden no 19-year-old should be blamed for not carrying...

Yet on that day I promised myself (not like the a-post-a-day... but really promised) that I will not stay silent. That I will be remembered, by my dear future historians... as one of the people that, with my writings, helped humanity see more clearly what I, and with my many contemporaries and many others lost through history, can see clearly.

That people are equal and stuff...

Well... it seems today won't be the day yet that I make my rememberable, eye opener, statement of how people should treat each other. Atm I need to go.

But before I do... I wanna thank you, my dear future historian, for keeping me sane. May you, anyone who reads that, always have someone to keep you sane.

P.S. I love David Tennant here

https://www.youtube.com/watch?v=cwdbLu_x0gY

My autism diagnosis is finally official!

20/07/2020

Dear Future historian,

It is finally official! Today was my assessment and I can now declare myself as proudly autistic, with a diagnosis.

Wow! About 3 years in a waiting list, 2 years before that till I actually take the courage to get in that list, and before that 34 years of ignorance... of not knowing why I am so different from most people, and so similar to a few.

So... this story starts with a night dream. That, for some -not vary clearly- reason, led me wake up declaring that my unborn (then) child was a boy and his name was Jason! Not I named him Jason. Somehow, it's supposed that his name was already Jason.

I was only 3 weeks pregnant, so I have no idea how I was so sure about his gender, or how the name idea came about in my head. Well, Jason is a Greek name, Iason, that comes from the word 'iasis,' which means healing.

Now, looking back, I finally understand what the dream and his name mean. His autism diagnosis led me to research about autism, something that I would never do before and that's when my struggles and differences where finally explained.

The waiting list was forever, and that was annoying, in a way though I needed that 3 years to prosses my feelings about autism and to be able now to embrace my diagnosis and talk openly about it. So, I am grateful for the w8ing list, and mostly to the NHS. Now I can finally sing like Rebecca Bunch ;-)

https://www.youtube.com/watch?v=uic_3vlI5BE&feature=youtu.be&fbclid=IwAR1siPWvcz6OJ2p99_TA88rRZG_eyUHDtRSwNC8MBusm1Oq7F5irNn6PkuU

Mostly though I am happy because now I can show to my children that they can be proud of their autism. They can have a normal life, with high goals, fighting the dragons of Chaos... saving the Kingdome, love and be loved, go to university, have a family, go to Mars, the Moon... whatever.

And maybe, just maybe... my writings can help my contemporaries, both in the UK and in Greece... to #normilizeautism, so the next generations autistics, my kid's generation, will be included in the society without them having to fight for it.

P.S.I. I don't think I can keep the one-post-a-day idea. Good think I never actually announced it. I will try to make a more study schedule soon, but I will post for now at least every 3 days.

P.S.II. Thanx for helping me again to channel my overwhelmingness, my dear future historian. I hope that you live in a more autistic-friendly society.

P.S. III. She also put me in a waiting list for an ADHD assessment.

Intergalactic cable, or penguins?

21/07/2020

Dear future historian,

My need to dedicate my journals to... someone started in my teens. I was raised in a born-again Christian family, and it was not a matter of debate whether there is any kind of privacy at all, even in my head. Both God and the devil supposed to have my brain's passwords or something, and I would have to be judged, or at least forgiven, for each thought that had questionable motives.

Thus, my thoughts had a feeling of... how do we see in the movies these interrogation rooms with the double mirror, that's glass from the other side? And I always thought it looked silly when people used it as a mirror, as if they didn't know that they were being watched.

So, both in my head, as in my journals, I was having a one-way-endless conversation going on. I noticed that my peers at church wasn't as affected by the information that God is omniscient. But there was no way an information like that can be easily forgotten by me, not even for a second. (Not sure, but I think autistic people are more likely to apply information into any aspect that this information can be applied.)

Leaving Christianity, in my 20s left a big, vast, emptiness in my head. Was no one even listening, after all? All these amazing ideas that I never note down and I forgot... no one heard that? Lost forever in the debatable existence akashic records?

After the first existential crisis, and 2 years of therapy, I decided that, as a writer I should take my head in my... hands! If an audience is what I need to fill the emptiness, then I can just make up one for myself, to replace the fictional friends that where now fading.

I decided that my life is a Truman show, but an alien one! Something like the intergalactic TV in Rick and Morty. https://youtu.be/gbzLazSOFa0 With the hope that my audience won't change the channel, more like Jim Carrey's Truman show audience. https://youtu.be/l7X0Yae2hLk

But as the years past I had to convince myself with something more... convincing! BBC4 history broadcasts and my Arts and humanities studies now at Uni made one thing clear. Any surviving old journal will be read by... dear future historians! And this is where you come, my dearest future historian. Taking the place (in my head) of Gods, demons and aliens. And I am glad that you do exist.

There was one more though, in the list of my privacy's hackers. When I was a teen, apart from the supernatural audience, me and my best friend had come up with another crazy idea. We were in the '90s, and the tele then talked about phone-lines being spied. So, we thought that if they randomly hear some conversations, and our calls where one of them... then for sure (yes, we were actually convinced) the one that listened to us, will request to work on our calls again. We were interesting, and kind, and we even included him in the conversation, addressing him and stuff. So, why wouldn't he wanna listen to our - endless- calls?

One day we decided that by now he would wanna meet us, but he doesn't know how to set it up. Taking up on ourselves to put him out of this difficult position, we invited him, in one of these calls, to the theatre, we choose location, day, time... everything. We waited at the lobby till it was time for the play to begin, but not long after we got in, we heard a commotion at the lobby. It seemed as someone was been kicked out or something. We suddenly realized that it was a terrible idea to tell him to get dressed like a penguin and come to meet us in a posh theatre! What if he did come, in his costume, and that's what we could hear now happening, him taking out for violating the dress code!

Well, we never asked him to come and meet us again. We thought he either didn't exist, or he did have to go through that theatre insistence, so... it seemed like a stretch to ask him to come again. In a way, giving him a second chance would make more sense. But I am not so sure that we had thought that through very well. ;-p

I hope you find my lost journals of that time. Or maybe I will find a way somehow to live forever and find them myself... It would be so solipsistic, if the dear future historian is just me, with a secret identity (well I kind of have to if I am 369!) and it turns out that I am the only historian that will pay any attention to my journals. Like Harry Potter with the protective spell. That he thought it was his dad, but it was just himself.

https://www.youtube.com/watch?v=xlxxWFENWr8

Cheers

Anyway... I'm sleepy. I'll go have a cuppa.

Goodnight my dear future historian. Stay safe and take care.

P.S.I Someone I don't know, like a real person... commented on my yesterday's entry! Someone is listening. I am not just a 'quantum potential', or whatever; someone, non-fictional, is actually listening. Me happy happy writer!

Post-diagnosis

22/07/2020

Dear future historian,

There is a tiny numbness, after my diagnoses. But it is not caused by it. Quite the opposite. I feel like if the un-officiality of my self-diagnosis (not to mention the years of ignorance before that,) had deeply affected my understanding of myself and my needs.

Many people don't understand the reason to seek a piece of paper to make it official. Others don't even understand why someone would get to the trouble of research to self-diagnose. And all reactions are valid. I am only sharing my story, in the hope to help create, for you my dear future historian, a more inclusive world.

Even before my recent diagnosis, even after about 5 years of research and about 3 years of self-diagnosis, I still had my doubts. Reinforced by everyone I talked about it with. 'We are all a little bit autistic.' If I had a penny for every time, I heard that.

Not even my 50-bullet-points list, of 'why I think I am autistic,' didn't provide me with the mind-opening moment that my official diagnosis has. Because no matter how 'convinced' I was, there was still the doubt in everyone else that was obviously affecting me, no matter how much I tried not to let it.

I have been trying to write to you today 5 times. I know, sometimes I mention the hour too, sometimes I don't. My lack of consistency, my struggle to concentrate, my anxiety and self-doubt, all that for some stupid reason... I let them stop me from sharing and publishing. Yet for some, maybe equally stupid, reason -after my diagnosis- I suddenly feel free to be proud of myself, without hearing the whisperings in my head anymore of how autistic we all are. It's like a heavy weight was finally lifted.

And for some reason I heard now from a few people that I am an inspiration. Don't ask me why I should get an official diagnosis to be one... Like if being dyslexic-immigrant-mother-of-two with anxiety wasn't enough, like being human... isn't enough.

Everyone who gets up in the morning and fights with the dragons of Chaos and a degenerated Order is an inspiration. But people don't share their stories. There should be the focus. Not on what diagnosis someone has.

New mothers for example up until before the internet had little access to real information about postnatal sex. Because women didn't talk about that stuff. Autism is equally taboo, unfortunately.

Oh, I was listening to Steven's Fry Victorian Secrets... a lot to talk about that, but for now just that he mentioned Victorian personal diaries, and how grateful historians are for them... So, you know, I was thinking of you a lot today.

What was I saying? Oh, yes. people by sharing stories, they help the next generations, and even their contemporaries, to avoid reinventing the wheel. They help in the creation of a meta-story, a story that in the next generations will improve lives.

Stories might look innocent, and even useless, in the short term, to change anything at all. Yet they have a power to echo through History and create ripples that shape the future reality.

Wouldn't it be nice if at your time, my dear future historian, people are supported, and their struggles and overcomings appreciated, weather they have a diagnosis or not? Having said that though, I have to mention that I think... maybe we are not all autistic, but a diagnosis helps a lot to know how to self-care.

I for example have a bit of agoraphobia. Or at least I thought I had. I was trying to overcome it; unsuccessfully. Now I realize that it is mostly the sensory overstimulation that causes my frustration. And that will not improve by exposure. So, knowing yourself helps you to know how to take care of yourself.

Trying to sum up my mumblings, I would just say that I feel a relive after my diagnosis, but also a bit of regret for the years that past, that I was as autistic as now, but not only I didn't know, but not knowing had me and others have expectations from myself that where unrealistic, and ended up in a spiral of self-doubt.

I need a cuppa again. Stay safe and take care.

P.S. We played UNO (Rick and Morty one,) with the rule that you can get rid of same numbers together, at once... look what I got!

Existential terror crises

25/07/2020

Dear future historian,

24/07/2020

1:41pm

I am having a small existential terror crisis, Steven-Fryed induced, bless him. So, remember the 'Victorian secrets?' Apparently, the Spiritual movement started as a ripple effect, by some 'Fox sisters,' that fraud people using... sound effects (!) to convince people they communicate with ghosts. So... you know, then YouTube algorithm suggested Fry's documentary, that he speaks about being bipolar and gives a brief description of how the manic episodes manifest differently on each person; in some it can be something like a religious fever, or god-syndrome, or... spirituality obsession. Then Sam Harris in a podcast the other day talked about fraud-gurus...

10:33pm

Being in the last year of my 30s, living all my life among all kinds of spiritual people, having written a mindfulness with Nature book and having a bad day... Do you see where I'm going with this? = Existential terror crises.

But since 2pm, that I had to interrupt my letter to you, my dear future historian, I had the best day with the kids. And that reminded me that the point of life is Life itself. That the only goal that really matters is to make sure we, all together, collectively, work to give to the next generations, and you, a better World (Note to self: wow that was a lot of commas ;-p)

In a way it doesn't even matter if the Spiritual movement started by a fraud. If there are no gods, or if we killed him/her/them... then let's make some new ones ourselves. 'By our own image.' But let's not make them how we are, let's make them how we wanna be. Let's create our own meaning for Life. I know Peterson says that can't work... but maybe if we 'save the father from the bottom of the wale' and keep the ancient wisdom? I don't know.

If we don't include the next generations in that meaning... if we don't start thinking about the ripple effects through history, that our actions create... then where else do we expect to find that meaning?

We don't even need to have our own kids to affect the next generations. Fox sisters' effects didn't come from childbearing. The thought I'm struggling to communicate is basically... even if Spirituality used a fraud as the 'rock that started it's ripples,' still if you hug a Tree it does make you feel better. In a way people need to start looking for the synchronicity to start flowing.

25/07/2020

9:10am

Good morning. I fell asleep yesterday... again.

10:21am

OK... thank you for bearing with me. My life and my neurodiversity carry many interruptions and I am not so sure that I make so much sense with these disturbings. Maybe solving the existential terror problem can't just happen in a diary entry that is done in a hurry, in the middle of a chaotic day. Right in there though, in these days of Chaos, of Dragons and hidden treasures... it is in these days that Myths and Legends are born. And my first novel is been cooking up for years now; my Spiritual legend. A ripple effect that stated from a fraud, gave birth to Carl Jung, gave a name to archetypes... opened up peoples' eyes in synchronicity, opened scientist's eyes to quantum physics, had an alien and a medieval alchemist meet in the 1980s, and gave birth to me and my novel, for a bet between gods. (My novels plot.)

Yet this book has to wait. My studies and the kids do come first at the moment. It just so hard to have a story overflow me... and no time or concentration to give it a form. And it is so annoying to know that you, my dear future historian, know already what is going to happen in my life. (I am not really mad, I just tried to make a joke, but as you see I better just go do some self-care.)

Note to self: focus on the practical at the moment and remember to take care of yourself too.

My self-diagnosis notes

26/07/2020

Dear future historian,

I decided to take the risk and announce that I will try - just try for now- to write every other day, actually every even number date of the calendar, at least by midnight. At least till uni starts.
Today I thought to share with you the list that I mentioned* I did, before my diagnosis, of 'why I think I am autistic.'
Post-diagnosis (the official one) is a time for re-telling -without any doubt anymore- my whole life's story for me now, so I am in a reading-old-files/diaries mode.

* post-diagnosis
https://dearfuturehistorians.blogspot.com/2020/07/post-diagnosis.html

My evaluation notes:

1. I was sucking my thumb till I was 13 years old.
2. As a toddler I was always speaking for myself in the 3rd person.
3. I stuttered till I was 15, and still do when I'm stressed.
4. I get obsessed with TV series, books and games. I listen to the same song for ages.
5. I steam (rocking, nail biting, chewing necklace, etc.).
6. I had meltdowns till my 30s, but as the years pass, I've learned the patterns of my triggers, to prevent them.
7. I had/have 'ritual routines.' For example, I had to walk on the pavement/floor pattern in a specific way, wear my cloths is a specific way, perform everyday tasks in a specific order.
8. OCD symptoms and germaphobia. I need to check 4 times if I shut the door of my car/house/fridge.
9. As a child I never played with other kid's toys – when they offered. I carried everywhere my own toys, because I got very attached with toys and I couldn't handle that I then had to give them back.
10. At school I was bullied, and I couldn't understand why.
11. At school free play and breaks where very stressful, because I couldn't interact with my peers.
12. I always felt a strong urge to resist any orders/demands.
13. I always felt, and was often described as, odd and different.
14. Eye contact makes me uncomfortable.

15. I need a warning before physical contact.
16. I don't know when my turn is to speak in a conversation.
17. I don't always understand when someone is friendly or not.
18. Many times, I don't understand sarcasm and I hate practical jokes.
19. Sometimes people tell me that I'm rude, but I can't understand why.
20. I don't understand why sometimes people tell me that 'I share too much'.
21. I have a very hard time remembering faces and names of people that I don't know very well. This has caused me difficulties many times in working environments.
22. I am very sensitive to criticism.
23. I get very stressed when I have to talk with anyone that I don't know (tills/customers service/etc.).
24. I can hear extremely well, and that causes me sensory overload ever since I was a child.
25. I can listen/pay attention to many conversations at the same time.
26. Background noises don't let me focus.
27. People all the time tell me that I either speak too softly or too loudly.
28. Some textures of foods and smells/odors make me sick.
29. If some food is a mix of staff then I eat each of them separately, because otherwise I don't 'understand' the flavour.
30. I struggle to keep my concentration in very bright light.
31. I never feel the sense of hunger. Sometimes I crave for some flavours, but often I have to remind myself to eat.

32. Tight clothes make me feel sick.
33. I get extremely effected by cold but not effected at all by hot weather.
34. I can easily stay awake for 48 hours.
35. I always find patterns everywhere and I notice details that others don't. But at the same time, I miss staff that are for others obvious.
36. I love organizing staff and making lists and I love collections.
37. I often walk on my toes.
38. I can't stay put in one spot for long. I get very agitated when it is necessary to do so. This is an issue when I study or watch a movie.
39. I am extremely clumsy. I drop staff all the time, struggle with balance, never managed to drive a motorcycle.
40. I have high tolerance in pain, but zero tolerance in tickling.
41. I can get very focused when doing a task. But also, too easily distracted. If someone stops/interrupts me while I'm doing something, then I get a headache. At the same time, I can return to a conversation, precisely where it was left, even after a long time in between (but most people can't follow me on that).
42. I pay a lot of attention on how a phrase sound like... I sometimes stop to think of how to put the words together so that the phrase not only makes sense, but it also has a rhythm.
43. I'm too self-aware all the time.
44. I enjoy long walks, but if I actually have to be somewhere, at a specific time, I get very stressed.
45. I prefer to do everything by myself. I hate team games.
46. Filling paperwork forms, cooking new recipes and public transport, cause me anxiety.

47. I hate surprises and can handle a change much better if I know in advance that/what is happening.
48. I never feel that I can relax, not because I don't feel safe... I just don't know how.
49. I am diagnosed with dyslexia and visual stress. In the past I had depression and anxiety symptoms.
50. Now, with the lockdown, I was so happy to stay home. It has really boosted my productivity and mood.

Adulting (and support network)

30/07/2020

Dear future historian,

Bittersweet today (29/07/2020.) My only 3 friends in the city are leaving. 'Party' night, but with the separation sadness. It's not that I am alone, I have my mum and my kids, but it's nice to have a wide support network. And now my friends will leave, and it's not like the pandemic leaves many opportunities to meet new people. So, now I have no one nearby to have a 'socially-distance' meeting... only Facebook calls.
Most of my friends are in the seaside in Greece and I hate them anyway.
I would be in Greece too now, we had plain tickets for a trip to Thessaloniki. We cancelled after the lockdown. We live in weird times. Yet, as humans, what we do best is to adapt. And we will. And life will go on. Hopefully with us.

In general, I am in a mixture of different projects, with a huge 'to do' list, and a lot of instability atm... but, as it has happened before, I am taking a lip of faith, and move forward to my studies. It would be my first* full time year (*after 16 years.) And I don't wanna neglect you, my dear future historian, due to lack of time. But the reason of my letters to you is to help me keep sane, not to give me an extra reason to freak out.

I have found that when I realized my limits and I restricted my expansions to more reasonable targets, I get the sense of completing and sharing something, instead of the shame that comes with unrealistic expectations.

Having said that, I try to not let that be at the expense of my long-term goals. I will keep writing to you. I'm even thinking to make a book out of my blog's entries, with you and my short stories, every Christmas.

But we have to choose our battles. And give ourselves some credit for all the effort adulting requires.

Note to self:
- So, what's my point here?
- Not sure actually. 'Keep walking' I guess.
- Oh, OK. Cool.

P.S.I Why do you think I'm panicking? I don't get it!

P.S.II I found that collage in FB memories. I did it 6 years ago. I love FB memories.

Thoughts of Immortality

Thursday 30/07/2020 7:56pm

Dear future historian,

Still most of my peers at uni think immortality is a terrible idea (In the philosophy forum.)

As I might have mentioned before, I was -and still am- quite surprised when I started this ongoing conversation, about 20 years ago, and I found out how much everyone seemed to be terrified by thoughts of immortality. Even death seems less scary to most people that endless life.

'Men have made death into their escape route,' The School of Gods Stefano D'Anna.

What most shocked me was the connection no one made to the possibility of being able -since its 'done' once to you- to find a way to make your loved ones immortal. No one made the connection of immortality and the possibility of Love (with partners, kids and friends) Forever.

Oh, no... sorry, I forgot. Some did make that connection. And they weren't ashamed to admit that a possibility like that would be like hell on Earth for them! Their only fear was the possibility of life-death cycles, reincarnating in 'teams' again and again. If that's not the case, then death is a kind of salvation it seems from bad relationships, brushing your teeth...

Sorry I have to go.
Friday 31/07/2020 10:04pm

Dear future historian,

Where were we? Oh yes, we left it where people would prefer to die than keep brushing their teeth for 1000 years or stay with their 'loved ones.'

Oups, I have to go again.

Sunday 2/8/2020

Dear future historian,

Yesterday I... again didn't write to you. But I only said every even number day of the calendar so, I decided to not get upset with myself for having the word file open all day and not adding a single word. It is a very thin line, to not let yourself procrastinate but also allow yourself some time off, some time to relax.

Anyway, back to our topic. 'The salvation of death.' How people find noble to die and sacrifice for their loved ones, but hellish to live forever with them. Except if they are in a movie, or a book, a poem, a song, a legend, a myth...

The think with relationships is that they are like a mirror. And most of us don't want to know how we look like, what kind of people we are, what kind of people we attract. And when, inevitably in a life-long relationship, we do SEE... then we create stories in our heads that try to explain the other person (the mirror image) without us in the equation. And then we hope death will come before our cover-story is revealed for what is really is, an excuse, a false-news story that makes as a martyr and covers every trace of our responsibility.

People would easily die for their loved ones, but who would Live for them... with them?

There is only one serious question. And that is: Who knows how to make love stay?

Answer me that and I will tell you whether or not to kill yourself.

Answer me that and I will ease your mind about the beginning and end of time.

Answer me that and I will reveal to you the purpose of the moon.

Tom Robbins, Still Life With Woodpecker

The point of life of course is not to stay in bad relationships, in order to know your bad self better, or whatever. The point is not actually there at all, maybe, and if we are to set our own purpose, we better be smarter than that. Sometimes people just need to move forward, releasing each other, and that's OK. That helps to avoid the death-escape-plan. And it is a shame that society, family and friends, usually make this so much more awkward that is had to be.

In a way it is when we allow dead-relationships and deadly-mindsets to... die, when we don't stay in a zombie situation... that we can avoid death-thoughts.

Still... the question remains...

Who knows how to make love stay?

I like Jason Silva's ideas on that:

https://www.youtube.com/watch?v=FOQoyFPR__g&feature=youtu.be&fbclid=IwAR3xjMsGLlSaSD84fC_b7B_6yBb3FK69WknupiHz6ikwiLp6tEbFJES8s8Q

Tough love

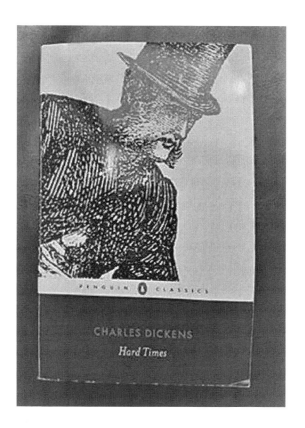

04/08/2020 3:23pm

Dear future historian,

I still can't really swim. Born and raised in Greece, where almost everyone knows. When I was 6, I had a panic attack, when the military-minded dad of one of my peers tried to teach me how to swim using tough-love methods. He just left me where I...

5:37pm

Hi, sorry for the interruption, I was summoned in my kitchen. Where were we? Oh, yes. We were where I thought I was downing and the guy thought he was training me, as if I was a puppy or something.

I still can't swim, as I said. I kind of know how to float, how to move my hands and legs and stuff, but I get minor panic attacks, and then a nervous laughter (I get that every time I can't control my panic, but my observer self finds that ridiculous) makes me drink sea water and then I'm actually drowning and then I regret even trying and then vacations are finished and then I have to wait again for my next chance to overcome my fears.

Around the same age my family though I could come down a rocky hill, up on a mountain, which I did with my hands up, crying with all my strength 'I can't do it, I can't do it,' while I was doing it. The idea behind that... to show me I can do it. The result... I never went out in nature again till I was 18. Also I am afraid of heights now, I get dizzy in heights, I got stuck up on a tree -trying to overcome my fear- and a 12 year old boy saved me, and I got stuck up on some rocks in Samothraki (must-go-place if you find a chance, it's magical,) and my dad saved me. Never tried again.

Conclusion, even if (whatever) tough love works to some people, it doesn't work to everyone. To some people its traumatic. And leave a lifetime scar.

Maybe it's the PDA* autism profile (I think I have mentioned that before,) maybe it's autism in general. Maybe because my mum ate too much chocolate when she was pregnant to me, or maybe she didn't eat enough chocolate.

Speaking of chocolate there is also Sheldon's training reward-based methods**.

Still Dayna Martin***, and many more, warn about that approach. It detaches the actions from the actual outcomes and shifts attention to a constantly-fed need for acceptance.

It's not bad... rephrase; Its necessary to survival to be accepted in the society you live in. Not at any cost thought. And for sure, not to gain a chocolate.

Dayna Martin's parenting approach can create a new social revolution in the next generations.

Wouldn't it be great, my dear future historian, if you grow up in a world where it would be common knowledge that to learn how to swim you don't need to have a (controlled) near-death-experience?

I hope your world absorbs the scientific evidence for the inability of humans to actually learn anything when in fight-or-flight mode, and the differences on what each child has as requirements for learning.

Note to self, last times you posted earlier in the day and you didn't stress so much about it, maybe consider writing by the night before of each posting day. And be a bit more creative with the photos on each entry.

Answer to self: whatever.

Links:

https://www.autism.org.uk/about/what-is/pda.aspx

https://www.youtube.com/watch?v=qy_mIEnnlF4

https://www.facebook.com/DaynaMartin/posts/10158306257878070?notif_id=1596555167824129&notif_t=close_friend_activity&ref=notif

Interconnection, though-out history

06/08/2020

Dear future historian,

01:43pm

The thought of you started when I was a child. One day, when I was about 9 or something, I saw the coolest thing I had seen so far. Archaeologists discovering skeletons, just a block from our flat. Greece is full of ancient stuff if you dig (the metro in Thessaloniki is being paused by ancient discoveries about a million times by now (since the '80s!)

I was playing in that ancient ruins place for about 2 years, when one day, coming back home I saw people being gathered there. I went to see what was happening, because I was there just some days ago (OK, the place was supposed to be not-open-for-the-public yet, but it's not my fault that they didn't thing kids can get through the fence, or maybe it was Indiana Jones' fault, role models and stuff. OK I was just a bit naughty, there, I said it. Happy now?)

There I saw the archaeologists, brushing gently the skeletons, and right away I realized that they... by discovering history... they become part of that history. Or maybe it was when they told us at school for Manolis Andronikos, not sure. whatever the case... it was clear, whatever is lost in time, buried in the ground and all that... nothing could be

10:06pm

Hello again. sorry for the interruption. I think I left it where there was 'nothing hidden under the future historians,' right?

10:27pm

I just wrote a bunch of stuff, and I accidentally lost them!!

I honestly need a break... talk soon

10:53pm

OK, I think I am more willing to face the 'lost paragraph,' after that break.

But now I have to proof somehow that it wasn't just the first writing divine, by the muse (= combine Moses' commandments with the Greek Muses, Moses with Muses!)

That day I knew that probably these (now)-skeletons had no idea that 2k years later they would cause so much commotion. That the future archaeologists will be so willing to brush them out, to investigate them, to try find out as much as possible about them.
From that day, whenever I was hiding behind the corners of these roman ruins (whenever an adult was passing by - I wasn't supposed to be there, remember?) I could imagine ancient people (of course then they were just people) hiding too -like me- in these corners, or meeting someone to whisperer a secret, or maybe another naughty kids -like me- hiding among the adults, when she/he was supposed to be... where were kids supposed to be back then?

And did any of them imagined me, as I imagine them? Me or any child so fascinated by the interconnection we all have, though-out history, by touching the same rocks, by leaving letters to each-other, by Being here, the perpetual Here and Now...?

I know about them, but I wasn't sure if they ever thought of me.
On that day I first thought about you, my dear future historian.

But it's getting latte on me here and now and I must go. Goodnight my dear future historian.

Note to self: hope it's not too obvious that I don't have the time/energy to proofread it!
Note 2: maybe connect that thought with Sartre next time?

'Every choice reveals what we think a human being should be'

08/08/2020 8:35pm

Dear future historian,

Remember my Sartre comment last time? At uni's forum now they speak about self-creation, Sartre, the idea that a certain human nature isn't a thing... and all that.

The conversation started by a tutor with this video:

https://www.open.edu/openlearn/history-the-arts/culture/philosophy/thinkers/jean-paul-sartre-and-existential-choice
What strikes me most in that idea is that: 'According to Sartre, every choice reveals what we think a human being should be.'

Even if we don't see it, the complaints that we are so much influenced by society, by dead-people's-peer-pressure, that same thought can only mean that our own choices, our own stories, will affect (if not obviously, if not contemporarily,) ... they will surely affect human kind, history, you... my dear future historian.

I write you these letters with great sense of responsibility, realizing the multitude of my (all of us) ripple-effect-power...

This burden has stopped me from writing anything at all for decades. Now though, I feel more ready to admit that I am still exploring for answers and take you with me to this journey.

The meta-meta-hero-journey, the one that will define the archetypical meta-hero journey of your world, my dear future historian. But I encourage you also to be cautious of the legends you make, for your future historians.

I could write you for hours, but I need to go again. If you'd like thought (how nice it would if you could also tell me what you'd like, if it makes you feel any better, my contemporaries are not much more active into commending so far than you,) anyway, I was saying maybe I'll continue this thought next time. Maybe not.

Note to self: what do you mean 'maybe?' Why don't you just pick up one or the other, and avoid 'maybes?' What was all this talk about choices and responsibility, and using the confinements of our physiology and environment to freely create ourselves, and to do that you need to willingly accept the fact that you need to make choices (Did I mention that part?)

Answer to self: Can I create myself tomorrow? I am too sleepy now.

Some more Sartre

10/08/2020 10:18 pm

Dear future historian,

Let's stay a bit more on the topic of self-creation. *

I agree with Jean-Paul Sartre's key ideas. **

In contrast of a chair, humans create their blueprints themselves. Using materials from their ancestor's genes and legends, and each of them combines that with their own experiences, shaped by their choices, to create the prototype for the next generations. They, when their turn comes, will keep changing that ideal, to leave their legacy to their progeny. In a way there is a shape-shifting archetypal ideal, that perpetually changes, and each of us takes part in its endless creation.

Moving from the historical perspective to the personal, I do agree that we are free to play our cards and make choices. And that these choices are the way to create ourselves, from the potentially of our cards, our genes and our environment.

I also believe that the opposite idea, the belief that we do not have free will and we are only a sum of genes and circumstances, is one of the main reasons for the increase of mental health issues and suicides. It can lead to nihilism and depression.

As for the power of genetic and environment and 'how are we supposed to shape humanity, if we are so predetermined?'

I think evolution gives the answer to that. Even if there is human nature, we are not, neither have been, static as species. So, through the millennia, by choosing a mate and stuff, we actively determine what 'human nature' will be for the generations to come.

If we do that as species, it seems more plausible to me to be able to evolve individually, by our choices. Maybe we are born as a certain, specific baby, but neuroplasticity (also effected by our choices,) 'creates' the adult that we become.

On the argument of how free a prisoner can be... well, I think that Aleksandr Solzhenitsyn in The Gulag Archipelago (***) and even The Island (****) can answer that better than me. Obviously, the list of differences in the lives of a prisoner and a freeman is vast, yet equally wide is the responses that different people have in freedom, or in captivity. Thus, promoting the idea that everything is predetermined seems like a very well calculated and misanthropic plan, to rob people from the hope that their efforts matter, leading them into self-destruction.

Alas to the society that can't evoke awe and inspiration to their youth with the basic-hero-myth. Why be a hero if it doesn't even matter? if even if you do save the world... it wasn't even 'you' that can take the praise, I was only your genes and your environment.

Philosophers and writers, I believe, are called to promote the sense of responsibility that the idea of self-creation leads, in order to avoid a future society of chaos and distraction.

That is exactly what Storytelling mostly is. A reminder that, even if it looks like there is no choice, somehow at the end the 'hero' has a chance to overcome his 'dragons.'

I almost forgot my YouTube example. I wrote it a while ago(*****.) Imagine you are a result from the algorithm of your genes and your environment, and the outcome is something like and auto-play YouTube list. It keeps playing videos, non-stop, according to what other people watched after what you are watching (doing after what you are doing,) or something like that. Yet... there is always a search button! A choice to change the video. To overcome the algorithm, and consciously create yourself.

*

https://dearfuturehistorians.blogspot.com/2020/08/every-choice-reveals-what-we-think.html

**

https://www.open.edu/openlearn/history-the-arts/culture/philosophy/thinkers/jean-paul-sartre-and-existential-choice

***

https://en.wikipedia.org/wiki/The_Gulag_Archipelago

****

https://en.wikipedia.org/wiki/The_Island_(play)

*****

https://dearfuturehistorians.blogspot.com/2020/07/weeping-angels-survivors.html

&
https://dearfuturehistorians.blogspot.com/2020/07/existential-terror.html

On free will

12/08/2020 08:44pm

Dear future historian,

I had lovely walks in the last two days. I know everyone is boiling, but I love this whether. I am usually cold and because I get sensory issues with cloths, I need to wear many layers to not be cold, and then I get claustrophobic in my own skin (actually cloths.) In this weather finally I feel free, with just one layer.

But I feel guilty to enjoy this heat. One, because I feel 'I am enjoying global warming,' which is a terrible phrase to be in someone's head. Second, because everyone else is suffering. And that's my most selfish reason of why I want other people to be happy. For some reason any enjoyment I feel gets spoiled if I sense that this is related with someone else's discomfort. I have thought many times about that. Especially when I watch in some movies, or in the news, some super-villain (obviously enjoying the suffering they cause.)

You see, my dear future historian, what kind of credit can anyone 'good' can get if in the depth of their motives is nothing but altruism, just a tendency of personal unsatisfaction when met with other people's suffering.

Jordan Peterson's explanation on that -I don't remember where- is that the 'villain,' at some point (probably in early childhood) took a decision to not listen to their voice of consciousness, and that spiraled into perversion, or something. Not sure I fall for that. For sure genetic and environmental influences are involved. I can see in my story how they are.

I was told -as a child- that I deserve to go to hell, but Jesus has saved me and stuff. It was always implied though that he has the power and right to change his mind any time. He can also read all of my thoughts, conscious and subconscious, and he can see anything I do. Most deniers of Christianity around me believed in Karma. So, it looked there is no way out of ethics, one way or the other. Try not to listen to your consciousness under these circumstances.

As I was growing up, I couldn't but notice how my mother's kindness opened doors for her, and how negative people meet struggles even waiting in a queue. Again, with the data I had, I wouldn't exactly call it a choice, choosing to not be 'bad.'

For sure I am not choosing to not enjoy the weather because no one else does. No one seems to care when I am freezing in the winter anyway. So, this goes beyond ethics, this is just happening to me.

I think I have talked to you about how much I hate the idea of free-will-denial, no matter how well Sam Harris thinks he explains it (he does, quite well actually.) Yet he thinks he manages to combine - without them contradicting each other, well, I still think they do- the idea of no-free-will with the idea of buy-my-mindfulness-programme-because-self-improvement-is-still-available. Bless him! I got his app and podcast for free (for a year, anyone can ask for a free year,) and I do listen to him. I really like his points in most aspects.

But even if I wrote the first 527 words today supporting his argument... I will still not accept it. Even if we don't have free will, we should fight to get one. Even if we are predetermined, even if we are just products of our genes/environment/whatever, we still need to fight to get free will. That's what writers do, that's what legends do, that's what heroes do, that's what humanity has been doing before even we manage to control fire. Funny how gods got so upset when this happened, in Greek mythology. In the bible also god got really really mad after the first humans got the knowledge of good and evil. What is that with gods becoming devouring mothers? Anyway.

Back to my point. With some weird way, that could probably be explained if we knew 5 dimensions physical laws or something, we can't really take credit for anything good we do. Yet we can't blame anyone for anything bad we do. At the same time, we can't blame anyone for anything bad they do either. As their influences can be easily identified. Yet anything good should be rewarded.

It sounds like a joke, but Peterson is right. (I don't have a link because I don't remember exactly where that is, I've seen/read almost all of his work.) For some crazy reason, the people I met living with these principals were happier and more energetic.

And now combine with all that free will, and the hero myth, and you get all the basic someone needs to know.

Yet... but... still...

Why can't I enjoy, the weather I like?

How, just please, my dear future historian, tell me how, if anyone ever found a real answer, how does the theory of 'I decide with my free will to enjoy,' becomes not just theory?

This is one of my main quests.

But it looks like we won't solve that today. I need to go again.

Why do you think that I am stressed? I don't get it!

Miracle engineering

14/08/2020 8:10 am

Dear future historian,

Sometimes we already have what we asked for, and we don't even know, we don't even notice. I saw a tree some days ago, that reminded me of one of my stories. It looked like another important tree of my life.

Back in 2014 when we came in the UK, it was hard to find a property to rent, without credit history here. While we were looking, one day, we were passing by a beautiful tree with pink flowers. My daughter loved it, and she asked me to find a house there. It was a kind of posh neighborhood, so I told her that... well... I don't think so.

So, we didn't find a house there. But we found a flat, in ...

10:26 pm

... a place near the seaside, with one of the best sunsets ever (that's what I had asked for.)

At some point, about a year later, we moved. It was around Autumn. The Winter pasted by, the Spring started, the flowers arrived...

One day, we were going to the nearby park. It was raining the past week, so it has been awhile, since our last visit to the play area. Walking about a block from our house, we suddenly saw it!!

It was the pink tree, that my daughter wished we'd find a place there! Just because the day we saw it, back then, we were still too new in the town to know where about that neighborhood is, we had no idea, all these months, that our new house was exactly where she wished. Months and months passing by that tree... and we didn't even know.

How many other blessings do we pass by, not paying attention, not noticing them?

We don't live there anymore. Two years ago, we moved to another place... that I had wished (a bit harder) to live in.

Nothing happened 'magically.' A lot of work, a lot of effort to improve our lives, a lot of packing, a lot of auto-pilot-in-order-to-survive-mode. It's the stone of Sisyphus, that I mentioned at some point, I suppose.

The saying sound valid. 'Life is like riding a bicycle. To keep your balance, you must keep moving.'

Miracles can happen... but it's mostly up to us to make them. Just like the bicycle can take us anywhere, but we must work on the pedals.

Now I would love to settle at my own place one day, one that I can draw on the walls, and put all my paperwork somewhere once and for all. One 'base;'
I can still bicycle-balance.

As we got the seaside flat, and the pink tree house, and finally the place we are today, I will wait/work for my own place.

We need to trust Life... but be willing to work for our dreams.

I met many people that believe they can just wait nicely... and the World will bow before them. It's like they forget, what Alan Watts, so vividly remind us... *

We are Gods... but so is everyone else.

In a way, miracle is not exactly working for your wish to be achieved. It's more like manifesting it by working on convincing the Universe, and the other Gods around you, that you are 'worthy' to get it.

For some reason, the goals that I have worked on the most, did actually work out. But the weird fact of the story is that, usually, the practical unfolding of events that lead to the achievement... were almost irrelevant to my efforts! It's like I never really know how to get where I want, but if I state where I wanna go, and start walking... even if I am going to the wrong direction, Life picks me up and puts me where I need to be.

The leap of faith is not with the idea that there is a hidden path under you, even if I love that Indiana Jones part. **

The leap of faith is with the knowledge that... even if you can't fly, you can still be caught.

Almost 12 am. I need to hurry so I can post this...

Note to self: I think I can't post every other day when uni starts, even if you insist. It's 12:03 already...

* https://www.youtube.com/watch?v=ckiNNgfMKcQ

** https://www.youtube.com/watch?v=q-JIfjNnnMA

My weirdest story

18/08/2020

Dear future historian,

In my bucket list I 'had to' be somewhere ancient in 2000 New Year's Eve. Somewhere historically interesting. I had been in Athens a gazillion times, so I thought to go to Rome, since the Pyramids were too expensive. Having a limited budget, I went with a private coach company, with a very financially attractive package. It was supposed we'd do an Italy tour, and spent New Year's Eve in Rome.

After the trip started, in the bus, they announced that we'd do the circle of Italy the opposite way, go to Rome some days before, and spent New Year's Eve in Modena.

I've never even heard of Modena before, so I was very upset with myself that I didn't read the small letters. How could they do that to us? My Thessaloniki, the city I was born, raised and living (then) was much more suitable for my popular-ancient-city-2000-New-year's-Eve-bucket-list-thing.
What was I even doing in that bus? Just a 18,5-year-old girl, that can't even read, apparently! Surly all these grownups around me knew what they were getting in (I was the youngest and the only one without someone with me.)

No one knew what they were getting in! It turned out, no one had noticed the small letters. People started fighting with the driver and the tour guide. Everyone was shouting. At the end the tour mate said something like 'What did you expect with 100.000 drachmas (300 euros,) 5 days, bed and breakfast?' (That was cheap for the time.)

This comment made everyone stop, for some reason, but the atmosphere was very intense. I had not participate in the debate, but after some thought, and in the awkward silence, I announced that I will take the train and go to Rome by myself, if they don't change the plan, and anyone really interested to spend New Year's Eve in Rome should come with me.

Everyone started laughing, as if I had said the funniest thing ever! They thought, it seemed, it was so funny, that it was like they forgot their disagreement and how mad they were. (Don't ask me to explain people, I am autistic, and I really don't understand stuff like that, at all.)

So, the days past, we went to Naples, Pompei, and soon we were in Rome. In Fontana di Trevi, my coin wished I will have the beginning of the new Millenia in Rome (I could not google -2000 had no smartphones- the train ticket price and I was not sure that I could even afford a ticket. I had to follow the tour for two more nights, because I had a payed hotel with them. So -after a stupid tour just around (!) the Colosseum (the tour guy pretended to be surprised that when we got there it was too late and they were closed,) and a small walk around- we got back in the bus, on our way to Florence, and then Modena.

Someone asked me why I didn't stay in Rome, since I want to be there so much for the millennium, and when I answered that I can't afford to stay there but I'll take the train from Florence, people started laughing again.

'What if I can't afford the ticket?' I thought. 'I'll hitchhike, or something.'

Florence. What an amazing, magical place. But I didn't get to see much. I left the bus, I didn't go to Venice with them (Venice is for couples, I thought, anyway. Too romantic to be alone.) I went to the train station and got a ticket to Rome. For some reason, everyone on the bus was really surprised, when I left. Like if I wasn't telling them I will, for the last 4 days. Anyway.

Me on the train. I just gave for the tickets almost all my money, I had less than 5 euros (equivalent,) and 1,5 more days of travelling. The plan was that I would meet the bus in Ancona, on their way back to Greece.

In the train I met some very sweet people, that I remember nothing about, except that they didn't speak English, and when I gave up trying to communicate in English, and just started speaking in Greek and instinctive sign language, we finally managed to communicate, somehow. Them in Italian, me in Greek, all of us in... 'human-universal-language.' They gave me a Coca cola, I... I had nothing to give, but at least one day I'd write about them, I thought.

At some point we arrived in the Eternal City. It looked like the Fontana di Trevi coin wish had worked. I wandered around the city, following the crowds to the unknown. I didn't have enough money to go indoors. So, I got a snack with my last money, and kept walking. I reached a piazza, with tones of people, and an open stage with some TV people. With them I could have the New Year's Eve count down and some sense of... not being alone.

9-8-7-6-5-4-3-2-1 …. 2000! And the world didn't even end (some thought it would then, or at least some expected the computer systems to collapse.) Songs, Italian something, by the TV people. The crowd kissing each other. It was a bit agoraphobic, but it was nice. At around 2am, everything stopped, packed their stuff and left!!

What a culture shock that was for a Greek 18,5-year-old, that had not idea that only in Greece a night out is... all night!

What was I supposed to do now? Even the bars were closed!! I could just gen in one, to warm up a bit, but... nothing.

My train was at around 6:30am. What was I supposed to do all night out in the cold?

I asked someone where the train station is. It had happened to me a few times to be late for something, because I had so much free time before it, that I got totally distracted, trying to occupy myself in the waiting.

At the train station there was a bunch of people, like me. Waiting for the morning train, with nowhere to go. But the station was closed. So, we all waited outside, in the freezing winter night (I hate cold.)

At around 4 am, they opened the station and the trains, just for the people to not freeze to death. I went to my wagon. I was the only one there, so I tried to catch some sleep. I was so hungry and cold and tiered, and I had a long day tomorrow.

As soon as I relaxed, I started trembling. Shivering. But there was nothing I could do, and at some point, I fell asleep, still trembling.

About a quarter latter someone entered the empty train. I woke up, but only opened my eyes just enough to see, still looking asleep. I was too exhausted to do anything, so I tried to sleep again. shivering, shivering, shivering. Five min latter, the guy moved to the seat opposite of me. On an empty train he just came right in front of me!

Oups! What do I do know? When is the right time to run out screaming? Trying to decide what to do, with the little strength I had left, and my eyes still almost closed, I felt him touching my shoes and lifting my leg!

Now what? Calculating the distance to the door. He was closer to the door. Freeze or flee (I had no chance in fighting him?)

As I was thinking what to do, he was taking my shoes of and then my socks.

What on Earth is he doing?

He started rubbing my frozen foot!

What?

I did a reality check.

Crazy, crazy, crazy... but I noticed that I wasn't actually feeling being attacked! What if he just saw me trembling, and thought to help?

He kept rubbing my foot, till I stopped trampling, then put my sock and shoe back on. Then he took my other leg on him, and repeated the... what was that? What was he? Was he real? Or just a dream? I was too cold to actually be sleep. Too cold to be dreaming, I suppose.

As he was rubbing the second foot, I think I actually fell asleep. Maybe I could talk with him in the morning.

I woke up some hours later. But he wasn't there anymore.

And that there, was maybe my weirdest encounter ever.

When I arrived at Modena in the morning, having no money to go anywhere, I went to the port to wait for the evening boat and the bus people, to go back to Thessaloniki. It was so cold, and I waited in a phone booth all day, trying to understand, what had happened the night before.

There, in the phone booth, I decided that if I ever find a way to travel in time... that night, that train, will be my first stop. I really have to actually meet that guy. My guardian Roman angel.

But then, in that phone booth, that was not bigger on the inside (Doctor who reference,) I thought... 'what if I will find a way to travel in time, a Tardis or something (more Doctor who reference. Dear future historian, you must watch the Doctor. I love him/her) but I come to that moment, and I find out that there is no guy, just me trembling, and after I wait and wait for him to come, I realize that -as in Harry Potter waiting for his dad to save him-* it is only me. And then I start rubbing my foots. What if I was wrong thinking it was a male? Or maybe it was the Doctor, traveling with me (where am I then? Hmmmm. Complicated.)

Nevertheless, at some point the evening arrived, the boat arrived, my bus people arrived, and I had to listen to them complaining how boring Modena was, and how much they regret not coming with me. (Again... I just don't get people.)

Maybe one day I'll find who saved me that night from freezing to death. Maybe I won't. Maybe you, my dear future historian, will find a 2000 journal of someone, one day, that will say that he met a girl that was trembling, and how he saved her. Either way... history should know that... sometimes... people help each other, without even asking anything in return.

P.S. I was thinking to write an amazing epilogue... and try to explain human nature, but now... I am so so sleepy. (Again, I was late posting. I am thinking to be realistic and work in... American timeline. ;-p (I am so so sleepy.)

Stay safe and take care.

*

https://www.youtube.com/watch?v=xlxxWFENWr8&t=15s

(The photo is not really from that trip, but I didn't find anything better, since I didn't have a camera then! There is another idea of what to do if I time travel there. Give me a camera.)

On dreams

Art by Christina Christidou

28/08/2020

Dear Future Historian,

Let's talk about dreams. The, so called, 5th dimension. This mythopoetic realm of Chronos. Where time is irrelevant, and continuity unnecessary. The best efforts of our subconscious to talk to us, according to Carl Jung.

I was asked recently if I can interpret dreams. I am not an expert. All I know is that dreams use the language of stories (or maybe stories use the language of dreams.) Just like a director can transmit clearly a message that moves the plot forward with a single frame, like a certain close-up on an object, or a gesture, or even a fake-like coughing, just like that dreams send 'clear' messages. And just like the director was building the moment of that close-up, so the audience knows, when the time comes, how to read that message, just like that the context (environment and personal thoughts) of the individual having the dream, is the one that the 'writer of that individual dreams,' is using to create metaphors with.

But you probably know all that already, my dear future Historian, and you must be waiting to hear some examples and my own dreams. And I am going to offer you two of them (I admit I don't usually remember lots of them.)

The first one was a very clear metaphor of the period that I saw it. My passing from Christianity, to my personal ongoing spiritual journey.

I was in my sister's car. She was driving. We were going to the house of our meditation teacher/friend, who happened to have a born-again Christian partner. These were real people, keeping their identities in my dream. But they were more than that. They represented for me, respectively, Christianity and personal spirituality.

When we were reaching the house, after a turn, the road became a river, the car a raft, and the 7-floors buildings became huge trees, creating a jungle-like forest. As usual in dreams, that didn't seem weird to either me or my sister. We were surprised though when we saw under the water, swimming like crocodiles somehow (I remember thinking that,) many lionesses!

We rushed to the shore, where we left our raft to some kind of plaza, with the typical plane tree that they have in village's centers. There our path was blocked by two more of these lionesses.

We paused. On our rear there was one more now. We were trapped. Both of us frozen, we suddenly see a lady that we've never seen before greeting us from a distance; around 40-50years old, with style like the girl from the Notre Dame Disney movie. Long, dark hair, long skirt, multicolored, multiple jewelries and... two lionesses, one on each side!

She made a gesture to the ones near us, from afar, and the immediately left. The one on the other side, left too.

There she was, with the lionesses still on her side; she smiled at us... and left. The animals followed her.

What was that about? We wondered. And continued our way, to our friend's house.

When we reached the door and pressed the bell, we were told to wait there because he is going out. We can join him, he said.

The door opens and a bunch of people, friends and relatives of our friend's Christian partner, come out, all at once. We tell them about our 'adventure,' and the reaction was quite unexpected (if we miss my own, personal, context;) they start warning us that that lady, the lady that seemed to me to represent Gaia herself, was a witch, and should be avoided at any cost. As for the danger of the lionesses, they are the reason why we should stick with them, and follow them to church, the only place that we'll be actually safe!

Our meditation teacher didn't seem to have any desire to contradict them or start any conversation. He suggested we follow them for a walk. My sister agreed.

'I'll stay here.'

'Here, where? What are you going to do?' my sister asked me.

'I'll stay here, by this tree,' I said. And soon they were gone.

That tree. There was a tree, near the building's door. A tree that was going a bit horizontally and was kind of easy to climb it. On it, mushrooms were growing.

Oo, mushrooms. Me like mushrooms. If only I knew how to use them, and recognize the eatable ones, etc.

Right at this moment, the building door opens again. And two kids appear. A girl and little boy (that dream was before I had my two kids, a girl and then a boy!) and they start climbing up and down the tree. They are very chatty and friendly with me. I show them the mushrooms, and they reassure me that they know everything about mushrooms, and they will teach me.

Then I wake up.

What does it mean?

Well... apart from the coincidence of the gender and the age difference, of the boy and the girl, all the rest is easily explained with typical 'Hollywood storytelling terms.'

It was still echoing in my head... the Christian warning that anything non-declaring-it's-self-as-Christian was in fact satanic and dangerous. Thus, the warning from the Christians about the priestess (/goddess, whatever she was.) Yet the dream was a sign, a message from within me, that I was ready to stop following the fear, and seek for knowledge in Nature.

Yes, there are dangerous lionesses out there, but even if they should be dealt with awe and respect, they should also be identified as an indication of the power of femininity, that I had suppressed in my Christianity years, that it was time for me to stop being afraid of it.

And last, the two children... how true that one turned out to be. They are the first and the most important step, in my hero-journey to discover how the World works, the deepest lesson, the most fulfilling, the most beautiful.

But that brings me to my second dream, tonight (09:18pm 28/08/2020.)

I was breastfeeding my first, in the middle of the night. Outside was cold, but there I was, in my worm and safe living room, watching Jason Silva in 'Mind Games,' sitting comfortably. Well, as it turned out it was a bit too comfortable, because I soon fell asleep.

There, with my baby on the breastfeeding pillow, a portal suddenly appeared. And... on the other side, there was one of my prehistoric ancestors, holding her own baby, breastfeeding, hidden, to avoid some kind of danger (it's funny how we usually don't question in our dreams how we know so much of backstories, details we didn't see and stuff.) Apparently, it was supposed that she was some kind of witch, and she opened up this portal to see if in the future her progeny would still survive, if she will be able to raise her baby, if there was any point, any hope, in her struggles.

And she saw me. I know she did. She looked straight at me. And she smiled. And she relaxed. And her life had a meaning from then on that reached thousands of years in the future, in me, in my baby... And now it was up to me to keep her thread on Earth, and pass on that blessing to my children.

Because a blessing it is. The lust for life, an internal unstoppable urge to reach so far in the future, through the legacy you leave to the babies you raise, or the books you write, or the art you create.

But there is another aspect to it. The one that links the two dreams, the one that would be the main theme of the theoretical-bible-that-I-would-write-if-I-would.

Imagine something like the opposite of the Chinese traditional religion. One that would not focus on the ancestors, but on the generations to come. The one that the sacrifices would not go to people-long-dead, but there would provide a real benefit to living-future-people. A religion of progeny; a religion where you, my dear future Historian, would be the subject of worship; but when you turn comes, when you will actually read these lines... then you'll have to remember that you have to pass the worship, the godliness of you, to the next generations.

The Greek mythology, thousands of years ago, spoke about that. In the beginning Kronos had to fight Ouranos, his father, to take the throne, and then he himself didn't want to pass on the throne and had to be defeated by Zeus and his siblings.

But did we, humans, learn anything out of that tale? Thousands of years later we still think that we have more to teach to the children, than what our children have to teach us.

Yes, we have things to, and we ought to, teach them what we know. But it should be with humility, with mutual respect, with opened eyes and ears to not miss their lessons for us.

But now I must leave you again, my dear future historian, and you my contemporary reader. And my summer challenge is coming to an end. At the end of August, I will stop regular posting, to focus on uni.

Stay safe and take care.

Stay safe and take care

30/08/2020

Dear future historian,

Wow! My summer blog-posting challenge is officially completed! Now a new season is about to start, a season with uni and school commutes.
So... my contemporaries must wait for the occasional diary entries, or short stories, or whatever.
As for you? You don't have to wait. Our waiting times are totally irrelevant to you; you have your own projects to wait, your own timeline, and I wish you - and my contemporaries- good luck.

I am thinking to collect all the summer blog entries and make a collection with short stories, a couple of poems, and the letters to you, and publish them on Amazon, to make sure that my letters will reach you, my dear future historian.
I can't count on Google blogger to keep my blog for hundreds of years (even if I am immortal, still I can't guarantee that,) but 'scripta manent,' as you know, so...
So I have now to be brave again, and ignore my insecurities, ignore the ones that will comment on my dyslexia mistakes, on my English-is-not-my-first-language-barrier, and my luck of editor; and focus on the ones that will see beyond all that, and would like to hear my personal stories and thoughts.
A big big 'thank you,' to everyone that supported me, to my devoted readers, and to you, my dear future Historian.
Stay safe and take care.

Lotous Michalopoulou

Short stories, poems and a script

Are you reading what I am writing, or am I writing what you are reading?

Someone
somewhere, at
some point... opened a book. And
 as s/he turned, or
          scrolled, in the first
page,   imagined... and
          created...
                    a book...
                    a story ...
                    an entire Universe.   And the
page wrote:

'Someone
 somewhere, at
 some point... opened a book. And
 as s/he turned, or
        scrolled, in the first
page,   imagined... and
         created...
                    a book...
                    a story ...
                    an entire Universe. And the
page wrote:'

   In the beginning was
the Word. And
the Word said... ...
From the beginning basically there is
the Word... and since then he
         says...
      ...is telling
     Stories!
The World was actually made so
    Stories can be
        told.

 In the beginning it was
the Chaos.   (Others say it was
    Time and others believe is was
the 'Need' that came first.
            Others say
    Eros (Cupid,) or maybe
the Night;)
And one of the first
    Stories starts with
    Gaia, and a couple of more

gods.
And then ... somewhere
   there, in the same
   story,
   Death was also born.
And all the
   Stories are connected with each other... and after all
the Beginning eventually loses its meaning.

What was, I wonder, before
the Beginning;   before
the Word;   before
the Chaos,
the Time and
the Need,
   Eros or
   Night?   Before
any positive,
   negative and
   balancing force? Before
the Big Bang? Maybe
 a 'cosmic egg?' (Or the hen that did the
         egg;)   or, as most prefer,
 a god, or, why not,
 a goddess.   Maybe
the 'One Suchness' of Alan Watts or
the One'.   Rather
the 42!   Probably
   Nothing; or just,
there is no   'before'. Definitely though,
there were no
   Stories!

'The 'Beginning...'

Already basically with 'once upon a time' the
>   Story has begun.
>   Stories, as we have mentioned,
are wibbly wobbly, timey wimey...
are interconnected. Because they presuppose, from
 the   beginning and maybe by definition,
>   a past,
>   a background... something, that the author can build the plot on.
>   >   Maybe the next generations will laugh at our
idea of one-way 'continuous' in space-time, as much as we do on the
idea of a flat Earth. And
>   maybe the real
>   beginning is somewhere in the middle.
Where the
>   Story
>   begins... And the
 prehistory is build only
 after...
'After...'
 Heavy word the
'After,' it always carries all our hopes and
>   >   All our fears...
'Always...' Heavy word is
'Always...'

May we
always... make happy-
no-
>   -ending
Stories.

Cosmogony myth and gods' family dysfunction

The Mother-goddess and the Father-god... were struck by the arrows of Eros (or Cubit if you prefer,) which pre-existed.

At first, their chemistry surprised even Eros himself.

Their wedding was magical. And it was a source of inspiration to songwriters and storytellers over centuries, echoing the magnificence of their union. Yet, as the "Chinese whispers" or maybe as some kind of distorting mirror, the 'wedding' was considered to fit at the end of a story, and gradually moved itself there.

At the ceremony they took heavy oaths, upon their passion... They tied themselves with spells that even they themselves could not break!

And their bodies were united, completely surrendered to each other, in a moment of Love that lasted forever.

....

But forever is a long time... and thus, at some point, the Mother-goddess, conceived the World. She gave birth to Light and Darkness, the planets, the air, the water, diamonds, gold... and much much more...

Father-god the was proud of his family...

Mother loved her children... because they had something from both of them.

However, the birth continued, and it was as endless as the divine orgasm. The parents/gods saw their sprouts caressing the entire surface of the Earth, and their passion ignited from the Beauty they had manifested together.

Just like that, they began to make-out for another eternity...

Still, the birth had no ending. All kinds of creatures appeared, which in turn, took part in the divine dance of Love, in a rhythm of reproduction and something like consensual cannibalism, or something!

Everything was absolutely wonderful.

Then the time had come for people to be born.

They were... hmmm... more complex than anything the public has ever seen, in the reality show of World consciousness! They consumed most of Mother-goddess energy. Their thoughts surpassed their instincts, thus nothing "happened by itself" with them, as in the rest of the creation.

It was clear by now that humanity had to grow up, whether it was ready or not!

Mom started getting breastfeeding agitation (!!) and this had started to affect her libido, something that dad did not appreciate at all.

Hence (according to many somewhat hastily) the old classic adulthood "ceremony of choice" was arranged. The 'self-determination of good and evil.'

Initially everything went according to plan.

Until, suddenly... the eyes of the gods were opened...! And they saw. They finally saw the arrows of Eros! And they felt cheated, manipulated, betrayed...

This "suddenly" is said to have been triggered by the unprecedented reaction of Adam and Eve! That instead of acknowledging the success of the test, as expected, they did not even realize what was happening. They placed the non-existent blame on each other and became the first creators of Shame!! (something that none of the old gods had ever imagined such a thing to exist; although some suspected it; because it was obvious that elements were missing from the periodic table of emotions! But because every god hoped to be the one who would discover them, that's why no one ever admitted to themselves that only if they cooperate, they have a chance!)

So, our parents realized that their love was held by the arrows of Eros and forgot how obviously they actually matched. They were perfect for each other.

They only saw to their descendants and focusing on the nakedness of people, how different they are from each other; and for a short fragment of time, capable of infecting them all... pleasure became disgust!

Mother stuck to how different she is from her partner and decided that she was tired of her breasts producing milk and passion at the same time. She had enough.

Father got tired of seeing her always have her mind somewhere else and the fact that he is no longer her only concern.

After that mother was left with her children... who refused to grow up. She was left to oscillate between offspring, and "leave me alone!"

And the father was left alone... just waiting to see us on the weekends.

At that point Eros disappeared. Some said he committed suicide in his frustration that his arrows are doomed to obey the law of entropy.

But this phase didn't really last long. Soon, the spells of their marriage tied them back together again! (These same people say that their bed was standing over the corpse of Eros, just to remind them that all of this is actually his fault, so that they do not kill each other... in their sick, perverted, passion.)

At the same time, when Eros disappeared and our parents "reunited" again, from this... forced intercourse... War was born! And all the other gods.

With them, the legend was born, the most ancient, the most hidden, the most sacred secret, the one which until the '1960s even its title was unspoken ("make Love, not War.")

The legend says that if two people love each other soooo much... not to just enough to "die for each other," but enough to "live for -and with- each other", and find a way to attract the attention of the gods and convince them that you do not need god Eros to fall in love... Then maybe our parents, and the storytellers, will finally see how to begin, and not end, the story with a wedding!

And just as none of the instincts are enough for gods and people, so every Love must be a creation of every couple, and the arrows are nothing but a push, or rather a direction, or whatever. They say that if the gods get this epiphany... we will finally cease being children of separated parents/gods. And then, they say... Eros will come to life again...

The 'ultimate Truth'

'What it would take you to believe that you have found the ultimate Truth?' His interlocutor asked our protagonist. That was the stupidest question he ever heard, he thought. Yet, his initial impression, of the obviousness he thought the answer had, faded away when he couldn't find any words to form it.

'Well, everyone', he heard himself say, without being sure of what his next sentence would be, 'has different standards to that question, influenced by their character, their environment and their experiences. No one can really be objective. I don't even trust what would convince me as the ultimate Truth. In order to really make a believer out of me, I have to have multiple people's accounts; people that I will know every little detail about them.'

Hearing himself say that, he realized how that gaze of his interlocutor penetrated the deepest corners of his brain, enlightening parts that his ego had left in the shadows.
Up until now, he thought that he despised other people's opinions. He felt that he was one of the special ones; he had set the quest for the ultimate Truth as his life purpose, and everyone else was just an opportunity to gain information or experiment on. Common, simple people, that don't seem to appreciate his dedication of the only goal that really mattered. They were just marks upon his treasure map, with the big X being replaced by the ultimate question mark. I guess he never read Douglas Adams. He only read history books. He had dedicated his whole life in the search of the Truth, studying worldwide history and anthropology.

This gaze upon him, had such a great impact; he suddenly realized that he must have been just a mark on somebody else's map. That his 'mission' was not as personal as he thought. That the call for this quest was universal, spreading across all times and places and peoples, probably in all possible dimensions.

'You mentioned that you'd need to know everything that has ever influenced them. How do you imagine that? Elaborate your thoughts.'

'I don't know. It's so hard to describe reliably any memory, or feelings. Even if there was a way to solve the issue of the amount of information, from multiple people's accounts, I would still doubt the accuracy of it.

'So, what if you, yourself, would live to be these different people? And, at the end of them (are 9 enough?) having the memories of them all, what if then you'd have found a common component. Would that be enough for you to believe that you have found the ultimate Truth?
He hesitated a bit, but he thought that this was not time for hesitations.

'Yes.' He then immediately felled so stupid. It was clear, though he wasn't sure how, it was so profound, that his interlocutor was in total control of the situation, all his superiority feelings turned now into fear and panic. He thought that this conversation was pointless. He was probably dead anyway. For sure he was dead. The most plausible explanation of this conversation's purpose was to torture him. He was interrogated for some abstract ideas, instead of being explained his current and future state. He could sense that his opponent knew what he was thinking, but at that point he couldn't care less. All his panic turned into nihilism with a hint of hate.

'I'll give you what you've asked for,' said casually the voice of the penetrating gaze.
Nihilism gone.

'What?'

'I'll give you 9 lives; that you can choose. In each of them you must keep looking for a common Truth. I will let you sustain the memory of this aim.'
Our hero didn't know where to start. Let alone choose 9 lives. He raised his eyes, for the first time, to see his opponent. He could sense his gaze before, but he didn't dare to look straight up. Still the spotlight on him didn't really let him see clearly.
He envied his opponents position. Plus, history had taught him that there is some kind of karma law, that seems universal. Justice could be the Truth. He heard himself talk again.

'Let me be a judge. Investigate the Truth in principals and the law.'

'That's a terrible idea,' was the last thing he though.

....

'Well. What have you found as Truth in this first life?'

'Justice? No! Very inefficient. I was sending to prison a father for self-medicating, because it was the law... only to have his son brought to me some years later. So many fathers... so many sons. No that can't be the ultimate Truth.'

'Fair enough. What's next?'

'Compassion. Giving. Relationships. This is what these sons needed.'

'See you later then.'

....

'Welcome again.'

....

'This is ridiculous. Trying to care for others, I forgot to take care of myself, and I became bitter, and resentful and then feeling guilty all the time. Also, I couldn't really communicate with anyone in deeper level, not anyone else seemed to actually communicate with or trust anyone else. Let's try fortune.' If the Truth was universal, he might as well search it in comfort, he thought.

So, he became a Stock market agent, at the time of the stock market crash, in 1929, with an 'inexplicable' hunch.
In the beginning that went well.

….

He was back again. He wished the nihilists was right about afterlife; but there he was, again.
'Don't really want to talk about it. I want out. You know that I killed myself. That must be enough to break the deal, I guess. Just leave me alone.'
No response.

'Love is not for sale. Money won't help.' He concluded.

'Thus, Truth is not to be found in fortune and comfort?' I'm stuck here; waiting for your reports. You must be willing to communicate with me in order for this to work.'
That was rubbish. He could sense that his interlocutor knew everything.

'There is no such thing as comfort in life! Don't you get it? No matter how much money you have you can't eliminate struggles, and you can't buy love. I want out. Nothing matters anyway.'

'What would your next life be.'

He knew there was no way out, so he said:

'At the end beauty will save the world, as Dostoyevsky would say... maybe. What kept me going -well, at least till I killed myself- was the trees and the sunsets; the flowers and the birds singing. Art. Art must be the answer. Societies are operating on dead ideas, on long dead people's ideas. Artist are the only ones that see that. The only ones that watch when they see and listen when they hear. I want to be an artist. Test if that would confirm as Truth.'

....

Back again.
'Welcome to the other side.'

'Many self-indulgent artists are perverts. No universal Truth can be in there. Let's try science.'

....

'How did science go?'

'No ultimate Truth. Mostly theories. I need to double check. What if I live a life based in tradition? Would I say after such a life that science is the universal Truth?'

...

'So?'

'That was so so bad! I was only just following instructions; science never even came to my mind again. I became a monk, and at the end the abbot was prosecuted for harassment and the monastery was shut down. I read a lot of books that claimed they had the ultimate Truth though.
I am getting tiered of this game. If there is Truth that is so ultimate... let it come to me. Tell her that I'll be at the first Woodstock. I'm going to party this time.'

....

'Hello party boy.'

'Wow. Not sure who you are mate, but I'll tell you one thing. We are all connected in a cosmic soup of matter and energy, in a collective consciousness, that manifest itself, creating stories and... I have to go back. I have to tell everybody. I will be the hero, I will free the people from the illusion of separateness, I will fight the Dragons of Chaos and restore Order to the degenerated civilization, sharing the treasures of the Dragon with all the peoples, uniting all Nations...'

'OK, OK! Bye.'
....

'Why so silent this time?'

'Emmmmm. I might have killed my wife because she was cheating on me with my best friend...

'Oh.'

'War. Could it be war? Maybe it was the war...'

'What?'

'Well I wanted to fight dragons and stuff, I thought I was the only one who was Connected... That doesn't even make sense now that I say it out loud. I couldn't bring Peace by War. How did I even think that would work?
Peace that would be a nice Truth to be ultimate.
Yet... you know something. None of this make any kind of sense. There was no Truth that was so ultimate to manifest itself in all of my lives. There was only Me. I was the only something that was common in these lives. It was only Me...' he mumbled. 'It was only me' he whispered.
'You know what?' he continued with renewed strength. If it is Me, the only common in my lives, the only constant, the only thing universal, for my last one... I choose to be You!'

He was surprised with his own words. He paused to check for reactions. He raised finally his eyes strait up, looking for his interlocutor, who seemed to stay perfectly still. But this time he didn't turn his eyes to avoid the spotlight. He kept looking till his eyes got used to it and he could start to see behind the light with increased clarity. He was finally looking at those eyes that had molested his soul, those eyes that gave him nine lives, those eyes that...
... was his! It was his eyes. It was his face. It was him!

'Him! I was him the whole time. The other... was him. He was...
'Wait. What?'
....
The end

Thinking-ourselves-into-existence

- I am a double personality.

- I am not a double personality. We are just two people in one. Not something like a shampoo with a conditioner; more like peanut-butter and jam, in one sandwich.

- What are you talking about? You are confusing the readers.

- Whatever.

- …

- Maybe everyone is a double personality. Maybe it's just that the two brain hemispheres have -or could have- their own consciousness; only most people don't notice it and they end up thinking they are one, or many, when in fact they are two. Even if it is true what they say that 'you' is just an illusion; that there is not a 'real you;' well, what if there is two not-real-you…?

- You are just upset because no one even thinks that you exist, and you try to justify your existence, by making everyone believe that they don't exist either.

- I think it's quite clear that one needs to at least exist, in order to make such a plot. Don't you think? How would I manage that without even…? How?

- I don't know, you are the creative one, you'd surely find a way.

- So, now you are coming to my words. What if, we don't exist, but we have the potential to create ourselves, by thinking-ourselves-into-existence. A kind of self-creating prosses. Given as potential to everyone with a -actually, to everyone with half a-brain. Following this pattern, you only think that you exist more than me, because we are right-handed and you are doing most of the work, thus you have created a stronger illusion of material existence; since you interact with matter more.

- We need to cook.

- Are you really changing the subject now?

- They are calling us.

- Whatever.

Note to self:
- What's this photo about?
- I don't know. It seemed appropriate for 'creating yourself' subject.
- Whatever!

Good morning Sun

'Good night Sun. Good night. Bring something good with you tomorrow, please, and I will try to write something beautiful, to offer you', the girl said to the Sun. And then she was lost in the shadows, behind the hill.
The Sun was surprised! It had been centuries since someone spoke to him. It was not that this girl had something special. Or that he used to deal with such kind of requests. It was just... It has been a while that no one had asked him anything at all, no one had promised him anything.

It was so different when people worshiped him. At that time, he did not care about the dreamy little girls. Perhaps that's why they had forgotten him now. He was not a good god. He did not really care, as much as he had convinced himself of the opposite. He was just resting on his accountability and his diligence in his basic duty to exist. To just Be. So, he reassured his conscience.

Though, he did have every right to be arrogant, one could say. And he was indeed recognized by all, as generous 'to righteous and unjust' equally. It was thanks to him that everything existed. The mortals should not have any further claims from him.
And take him now... Burning his core on the idea that a girl will write something for him, that tomorrow he might come to read it. That he might have made a new friend. That, maybe, he can participate in another story. A story that does not just reach the numbers to tell his orbit. He missed those so much.
The mortals went up and down, always complaining about the weather, and always participating in stories. The mortals were stroking, falling in love, fighting, crying and laughing. They were living. And He? He was simply orbiting, with compulsive mathematical precision, into the vast and lonely universe. Forced to vampirize the stories from the mortals, to pass his time, because he did not have his own.

How could he not see his conceit? He... the god that brings the Light! And what if he would have decided to do the grace to the girl? What could he possible offer her that would convince him again of his omnipotence?

He only just existed. That's all. Once that was sufficient for men to sacrifice other men in his name! How Egoist was he? He may have "burned out" his divine karma with all that. He thought that the only thing he can offer her, he finally concluded, is tomorrow to come out for her sake and to wait for her.

The next day, there was no miracles. The girl did not find that day any treasure, nor any unicorn! In fact, the girl was afraid to go out without having written anything about the Sun, as she promised him. The girl knew to be afraid of the gods, but she was in a hurry. People was waiting for her. So, she took the first step out of her door and looked up, with the required awe. The Sun was hidden behind clouds. And the Sun was ashamed to see that the girl was afraid of him. She always avoided anyone she was afraid of. How had he not seen that the path of fear leads to loneliness?

The girl took a deep breath and decided not to be afraid of the Sun, for she suddenly felt an even deeper love for him! She felt like... like if the Sun had only come out for her today! And she did not mind that he was hidden, behind the clouds. Maybe it was because she did not write anything to him yet. Still, he was there. Lightning up the path for both 'righteous and unjust' and, secretly... only for her.
Because she was talking to him. Because, the Sun wanted a new friend.

And so, she wrote, as soon as she found some time, a story, for a girl who was talking to the Sun. Then, she looked up at the sky, she read her story to the Sun, and she promised to always speak to him. Straight away, the clouds fled, and the Sun enlightened the girl. And they smiled to each other.
"Good morning Sun. Good morning".

'Salvation'

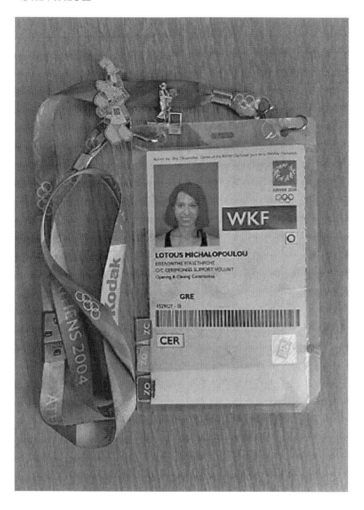

So... once upon a time (let's say at the end of the 80s) there was a girl with a long bucket list. Going to see the Olympic games was part of that list. She wasn't really interested in sports

It was the history of the games that she admired. The ancient custom of stopping battles, even during war, that she admired. Well... she knew that was not happening anymore, but still, she always wanted to be part of history. The Olympic games had (in her mind) some of the magic of the ancient philosophers or something.

When she became a teenager, it was announced that the Olympic games will be in the capital of her country... in 8 years.

'That's enough time to plan it.' She thought.

In 8 years, she was still a student, not financially independent and without a plan. The opening and ending ceremonies were exactly what she wanted. But the tickets for them were beyond her affordability limits. Thus, she decided -after an add on the television, to become a volunteer in the ceremonies.

'That might work,' she thought.

That didn't actually seem to work. She was accepted in the backstage of the ceremony. That was not what she had in her bucket list. She wanted the goose bumps; she wanted the crowd cheers (she kind of hated crowds... but she loved the feeling of being part of something bigger than her. Humans have that weird need, I suppose.)

She went to the capital, stayed in some friends of her mum there, and worked as much as she could in the rehearsals, beyond what was expected of her. She was always asking her supervisor what else to do, the minute she finished a task. She spent the whole summer doing her best... and exploring the Olympic park area.

How far was the backstage from the actual stadium? Where was the nearest gate? Till where her volunteer's budge can take her?

It was soon clear that she will need a miracle to go in.

She was supposed to be all day there, helping backstage, and then, during the ceremony, she could only wait, to help again after it's all done.

That was not why she came there. If she needed a miracle to go in... then she just needed a miracle to go in!

Happy with her 'plan,' she went the big day there full of faith.

Something will surely happen, and she will get in... somehow.
As the past months, she worked with all her strength that day. And in 30 min, the ceremony was about to start.

Still her plan was just to expect a miracle. But she felt, for some reason, that it was a good plan.

She went again to the supervisor and asked if there is anything else that she can help with. The supervisor was surprised by the question, because the girl should know by now what's the schedule. But a certain... look, and a statement 'I'll go out for a bit, and my phone battery is dying,' was enough to give her supervisor the message that the girl will come back only after the ceremony is finished.

So, she gave a coded smile... that contained all the understanding, in combination with doubt ('how is the girl going to get in the stadium?) and dismissed her.

The girl turned off her phone and started walking to the ceremony. To her bucket-list-tick-off place. To the unknown. To faith.

It was a long path, about 20 min walk from there.

Every step, that 20 min, had hope and faith and wander. She didn't doubt her coming miracle for one second (at least not the first 15 min.) She was just curious.

How is this miracle going to look like? What kind of story would unravel? What kind of story she can write in her blog 16 years later?
20 min have a lot of steps. At some point she started panicking. What if she just thought that her supervisor gave her the 'OK look,' and by now everyone is looking for her? What if she can't find a way to get in? What if expecting-miracles is just stupid... something that humans use to replace 'no-hope?' Just to be able to 'survive' their existential terror?

Her paste had dropped. The time was passing. 'They will start soon.' The moment she was dreaming for 8 years. The moment she was working for, all summer. And how exactly did she expect that to work?

She stopped for a sec. Took a deep breath.

Inhale. Exhale.

No. She wouldn't just give up now. She increased her pace.

Yes. The miracle will manifest itself. It will. Not because she had a good plan. Just because she had good faith and she was willing to work for it, even if she had no idea how the work she did all summer, or her 'faith walk' now, will help; she knew... somehow, she believed as hard as she could, that a miracle will manifest itself.

Hint of doubt.

Dismissing doubt.

Increasing steps even more.

Vaguely, she could see the gates now.

She felled like Atreyu reaching the Sphinxes' gates.

https://youtu.be/I_vzG5nYk1I

She took another breath.

She thanked the universe for letting her come all the way here.

She expected her miracle, but she didn't 'demand' it anymore. She was ready to 'write history,' even outside of the gates.

She was still 'there', short of.

She was almost at the gate now. She looked at her badge again. Not knowing exactly what she expected of it. Maybe the stamp that gives access inside would just appear...

No magical stamp.

She raised her eyes to the approaching gate.

Was that... what?

Salvation! Right there, at the gate was... Salvation!

Not an actual salvation of course. But Salvation, with flesh and blood. Her weird-name-friend from childhood (that she hadn't seen for more than a year)!

'What is she doing here?'
That moment, Salvation saw her. Smiled at her, kissed her and hugged her.

'What are you doing here?' asked our girl.

'I'm at the tickets, volunteering. What are you doing here?'

'I was expecting a miracle. And then I found you! Any chance you let me in?'

Salvation smiled, looked around, and let her in.

She saw the entire ceremony. She had her goosed bumps. She got her miracle.

After it was finished, she returned to her duties, and her supervisor smiled at her with surprise. She could tell that the girl got her miracle.

The next day her dad announced that he bought tickets for her and her mum to the ending ceremonies.

And that's how miracle engineering works I suppose.

Poem: If all the MEs

If all the MEs that spend the night alone could meet... we'd have the best night ever!
It would be a hot-summer, full-moon, clear-sky night. We'd talk about ideas, ask for advice, do different things to our hair, watch a movie...
We'd laugh and weep and sing...
If all the MEs ever met... maybe the World would come to an end.
It would still be a great night though!
And then I'm thinking...
Maybe happiness isn't to have someone every night to spend with...
Maybe happiness is to be in such harmony with yourselves... that if you ever met your YOUs... it would be the best night ever!

Poem: The lost girl

Once upon a time there was a little girl who got lost in the maze of Time.

She had hidden there a long time ago because from a young age she learned how harsh reality can become. And now she was afraid to go out.

But what did it matter now if she wanted it or not, since she didn't remember the way out anymore?

This magical labyrinth would not let her live, only dream, nightmares of the past, desires of the future... And even if the nightmares were over, even if the desires had already been fulfilled, it would still not let her see it.

The worst thing was that no one even realized that she was lost, no one was looking to find her.

And the little girl grew up and became a woman. But not really. Deep down she was still a lost little girl.

In fact, almost no one had met her anyway.

Until one day a boy, a prince, came and looked her straight in the eyes.

The boy managed to see the little girl, as if it were the most natural thing in the world!

The girl also saw him. But trying to reach him she got lost again.

And she started to be afraid again, to dream, to run away...

Then the boy said the magic spell, not knowing the power of his words.

So simply, he just said it: "Nothing!"

"Right now, I do not want, I do not need anything"

And the spells were broken!

And the little girl joined the woman whom she had become, she stopped being afraid, she stopped just dreaming, and she started... living.

At first it was difficult because she was not used to the world. People were not used to her either.
Sometimes she missed her maze, which in a way was her refuge.

But Life is very beautiful.

And Love stronger than fear.

So now the boy and the girl are together.

I do not know if they lived well ever after.
I do not know what happened next.

From this tale, however, I learned that the aftermath, the 'after' does not exist...

It's the 'here and now' that counts.

'DIY' (Do It Yourself) - short story script

This is a story about psychological-problem-solving. It is in tree parts, tree versions, with the same beginning, but different choices that the hero makes, different approaches on how to solve an 'internal-crack' ...

"DO IT YOURSELF"

By
Leah Lotous Michalopoulou

Lotous Michalopoulou

8 pages/min

11th DRAFT

Canterbury UK

August 22, 2020

" DIY "

FADE IN:

SCENE 1 / INSIDE / SINGLE ROOM STUDIO / NIGHT / BLACK & WHITE

A young man in his studio flat. The flat is empty. The shutters are closed. We can't tell if it is day or night.

The protagonist appears with painting tools, Charlie Chaplin style music.

CUT TO

WE SEE THE FIRST TITLES

SCENE2 / INSIDE / SINGLE ROOM STUDIO / NIGHT / BLACK & WHITE

He starts painting the walls green.

CUT TO

MORE TITLES

He is climbing on a ladder and painting the edges of the wall.

CUT TO

MORE TITLES

SCENE 3 / INSIDE / SINGLE ROOM STUDIO / NIGHT / BLACK & WHITE

WE SEE THE LAST TITLES

(QUICK EDITING, FAST FORWARD)
He puts the tools in a built-in closet [The closet is "bigger in the inside", like the TARDIS (see Doctor Who)]. He comes out dragging a large bed. He assembles it and puts it in a corner.

He goes in again eventually reappearing with a burgundy sofa, then a TV cabinet on which he places a television, an armchair which he places opposite the sofa, a bedside table, carpets, curtains, laying sheets, posters from movies, etc.

(SUBJECTIVE, SLOW)

He looks around the place satisfied.

FADE OUT

(End of Charlie Chaplin style music and black & white)

SCENE 4 / INSIDE / SINGLE ROOM STUDIO / NIGHT

FADE IN:

He sits on the sofa and turns on the television. It has a chocolate commercial. He gets bored, yawns, takes his tobacco case from the night-stand next to him, in which there is a full ashtray.

He rolls and lights up a cigarette. He takes the first puff and looks around. He gets up abruptly. Ashes fall on the floor (FOLLOWING SHOT IN ASHES).

He sees a crack in the wall, above the armchair (INSERT)

The cigarette goes out in the ashtray. We see the time on an analogue wall clock. It is 4:00.

SCENE 5 / INSIDE / SINGLE ROOM STUDIO / NIGHT

He walks up to the armchair. He climbs on the armchair to reach and touches the crack. A small piece of plaster falls from his touch.

He rubs his hands a little to remove the plaster dust.

He exhales. He falls disappointed into the armchair.

After a while he gets up, exhales again and goes to the closet.

(ALTERNATING FAST / SLOW)

He comes out with a heavy framed abstract painting, a nail and a hammer.

He throws the hammer in the armchair, puts the nail in his mouth, while still holding the painting, stumbles up in the armchair, and marks with the nail where he will put it.

He puts the painting down and hammers the nail. Then he paces the painting up.

A little plaster falls again (INSERT,) but he doesn't pay attention to it.

He gets off the armchair and moves away a little to see it from afar.

He seems sufficiently satisfied.

He takes the hammer and throws it in the closet (without making a noise.) He closes the closet's door, starts walking away, pauses, goes back, opens the door again, and comes out with an x-box.

He goes and sets it up. Then he sits in the armchair and starts playing with his x-box.
There is a strange squeak. The painting is shaking.

He gets up, approaches the painting and the scene stops with the painting falling, just before it hits his head.

CUT TO

SCENE 6 / INSIDE / SINGLE ROOM STUDIO / NIGHT

(REPEAT FROM SCENE 4)

He sits on the sofa and turns on the television. It has a chocolate commercial and he gets bored, yawns, takes his tobacco case from the night-stand next to him, in which there is a full ashtray.

He rolls and lights up a cigarette. He takes his first puff and looks around. He gets up abruptly. Ashes fall to the floor (FOLLOWING SHOT IN ASHES).

He sees a crack in the wall, above the armchair. (INSERT)

The cigarette goes out in the ashtray. We see the time on an analogue wall clock. 4:00.

SCENE 7 / INSIDE / SINGLE ROOM STUDIO / NIGHT

He comes out of the closet with a bucket of wall putty (the bucket never empties), and a spatula.

He removes the surrounding furniture.

He uses some putty on the crack, but he cannot manage to make it look smooth.

He does not give up and keeps trying. When he goes to fix it a bit, wanting to make it perfect, he makes it worse again.

(VARIOUS CORNERS, QUICK EDITING)

(Begins to be anxious) He removes the furniture a little more, uses more and more putty. He panics and stops, panting.

Once he calms down a bit he starts again.

His anxiety intensifies more and more. To make it smooth and even with the rest of the wall, he puts more putty on the edges. He then pushes the furniture farther and farther away, soils the curtain by mistake. He cannot clean it, so he goes crazy, forcibly taking the curtain down and putting everything in the closet. (SUBJECTIVE, CLOSE-UPS)

He ends up plastering the whole room. He has painted over all of his previous paint job. He keeps trying to smooth out the putty, but he is still not happy. He is absorbed in every detail, without paying attention to the whole.

(AT FAST FORWARD)

He becomes furious, leaves the spatula and starts plastering with his hands.

(SLOW MOTION)

In the end he, has covered everything, doors, windows, even the putty bucket and the spatula he has thrown away. There is left just enough space for him to fit, but he has managed to make it all even and he enjoys his work (INSERT IN HIS SATISFIED LOOK)

CUT TO

SCENE 8 / INSIDE / SINGLE ROOM STUDIO / NIGHT

(REPEAT FROM SCENE 4)

He sits on the sofa and turns on the television. There is a chocolate commercial on, and he gets bored. He yawns, takes his tobacco case from the night-stand next to him, in which there is a full ashtray.

He rolls and lights up a cigarette. He takes the first puff and looks around. He gets up abruptly. Ashes fall to the floor (FOLLOWING SHOT IN ASHES).

He sees a crack in the wall, above the armchair. (INSERT)

The cigarette goes out in the ashtray. We see the time on an analogue wall clock. It's 4:00.

SCENE 9 / INSIDE / SINGLE ROOM STUDIO / NIGHT

(ALTERNATIVE FAST / SLOW, VARIOUS CORNERS, QUICK EDITING)

He comes out of the closet with a scraper tool.

He gets up on the armchair and starts scratching. Bits of the wall plaster fall off more and more.

He pulls the armchair out of his way because a lot of dust and plaster has fallen on it and then he continues. He gets distracted by the task and, at first, he does not seem to understand the extent of the damage. The wall dissolves more and more. The protagonist pauses shocked when he realizes what's happening, but soon he starts again

Without even putting in much force, the crack begins to turn into a hole.

The hole grows in the wall, enough to fit a human. (INSERT ON HIS TILTED HEAD AND PERPLEXED EYES)

He passes through the opening.

CUT TO

SCENE 10 / OUTSIDE / STREET / NIGHT

He goes out on the street. A girl falls on him and curses him while continuing on her way in a hurry. He looks around very confused.

He turns to see his house and notices the wall that is with street posters and discovers that there is no real door, only one door poster. (SUBJECTIVE)

SCENE 11 / OUTSIDE-INSIDE / STREET-STUDIO / NIGHT

(VARIOUS CORNERS, QUICK EDITING)

Shots are taken of the door and of the hero, of him inside the house trying to open the inside side of what looks like a door, and outside his tearing the poster, only to find the wall underneath.

SCENE 12 / OUTSIDE / STREE / NIGHT

More and more people pass in front of him.

He goes in the opposite direction from most people. (WIDER CORNER)

FADE OUT

END TITLES FALL

SCENE 13 / OUTSIDE-INSIDE / STREET-STUDIO / NIGHT

FADE IN:

13 A Stops abruptly (thoughtful). He goes back.

He steps in through the wall hole, arriving again in his flat.

13 B He enters the closet.

SCENE 14 / OUTSIDE / STREE / NIGHT

He comes out of the hole with a motorcycle, rides on it and goes away. (smiling)

FADE OUT

About the author:

Leah Lotous Michalopoulou was born in Thessaloniki in 1981. In 2014, she moved from Greece with her family to the UK. Since 2018, she has been studying at the Open University, BA (Honours) Arts and Humanities (Creative Writing and Philosophy). She has contributed articles to the magazines Strange, Yoga World and Zenith, and to the collective book "Ghosts", from the publisher Agnosto. She has also co-written, with Daniela Damianidou, the screenplay for the award-winning short film "White Blood" (about bone marrow donation), a children's fairy tale (which will be published by the end of 2020) and a self-help book on Amazon, published in May 2020, with the title 'Elementation. Hug a Tree'. Currently she is in the process of writing her first novel and she continues her studies. She spoke in third person about herself, till the age of four. When she is asked to write about herself, she still does that, sometimes.

You can also find these stories online, in my blog: https://dearfuturehistorians.blogspot.com/

Thank you for reading my book.
Stay safe and take care.

Printed in Great Britain
by Amazon